Best Kept Secrets

For my first & great publisher, Bob Nielsen, with thanks and love,
Pat Krauel

Best Kept Secrets

STORIES

Pat Krause

Coteau Books

All stories © Pat Krause, 1988.

All rights reserved. No part of this book may be reproduced in any form or by any means without permission, except by a reviewer, who may quote brief passages in a review.

These stories are works of fiction, and, with the exception of "Webs" noted in the acknowledgements, any resemblance to persons living or dead within them is coincidental.

The lines on p. ix from "The Women in the Family" by Judith Krause are reproduced from *What We Bring Home* (Coteau, 1986) with the permission of the author. All rights reserved.

Cover illustration: "Sunday Sweaters and Orson Welles" by Elyse Yates St. George. Reproduced courtesy of the Saskatchewan Arts Board Permanent Collection.
Backcover photograph courtesy of Patricia Holdsworth Photography.
Design by Joyce Sotski.
Typeset by Type Systems, Regina.
Printed by Hignell Printing, Winnipeg.

The author thanks members of the Prairie Factor — Geoffrey Ursell, Barbara Sapergia, Lois Simmie, Bob Currie, David Carpenter and Byrna Barclay — for their help and encouragement over the years. She also wishes to thank the Saskatchewan Arts Board, the City of Regina Arts Commission and the University of Regina for writing grants they awarded to her. Special thanks to Bob Currie, editor of *Best Kept Secrets*, for the time he gave up from his own writing to help prepare this collection of stories.

The publisher gratefully acknowledges the financial assistance of the Saskatchewan Arts Board, the City of Regina, the Canada Council and the Department of Communications in the publication of this book.

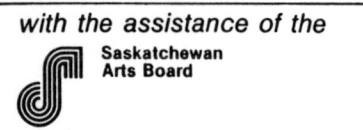

Canadian Cataloguing in Publication Data

Krause, Pat, 1930-

    Best kept secrets

    ISBN 0-919926-83-5 (bound) - 0-919926-84-3 (pbk.)

I. Title.

PS8571.R28B4 1988   C813'.54   C88-098142-3
PR9199.3.K62B4 1988

Editorial Offices:	Distribution:
Suite 209, 1945 Scarth St.	Box 239, Sub. #1
Regina, Saskatchewan	Moose Jaw, Saskatchewan
S4P 2H2	S6H 5V0
(306) 352-5346	(306) 693-5212

For Frank, Jim, and the women in the family, especially my mother, Florence Wilson Blair Warriner

Contents

I Secrets

Best Kept Secrets 3

Star Bright 17

Vital Statistic 29

Playboy 37

In The Middle 47

Second Sight 57

II Webs

The Lookout Stone 71

Aunt Hobby 83

Sudden Squalls 95

Just Another Midnight Attraction 113

The Water Ballet 125

Webs 135

---

*After breakfast, the women in the family
take their coffee and sit in the sun
on the wide stone steps....*

*The women talk incessantly.
Even the ones who aren't there
make their presence felt.*

Judith Krause, "The Women In The Family",
What We Bring Home, (Coteau Books, 1986)

I

Secrets

Best Kept Secrets

David Nathan Kaufmann: not gone, but forgotten for so many years. Born May 1, 1931 — a Taurus, the most popular children of the zodiac. They are the gentle bulls who do not fight unless they are tormented beyond endurance.

And me: born in the same year as David under the sign of Aquarius. We're supposed to be the most loyal children under the stars. But each sign has its opposites. Gradually, not remembering David became a comfortable habit, one that let me keep believing in lived-happily-ever-after endings.

It's no excuse, but forgetting David was what Aunt Enid and Uncle Nate had seemed to want us to do. They would cut any inquiries dead with, "Fine, thank you. He'll be just fine. Thank you." And their eyelids closed down tightly, an unspoken Amen, letting anyone see that further questions would be considered an unforgivable breach of faith and good manners.

But something was odd about the way Aunt Enid and Uncle Nate held their heads during those few silent seconds after one of them had replied. They bent their heads back instead of bowing them. That was it: a blind gaze upwards that made them appear more vulnerable than proud. I think now, they saw an ending it has taken me too long to accept.

A long time ago, Olga, the maid who had been at David's since before he was born, told David and me stories about life in the Old Country that had endings I never accepted. I was staying at David's. My parents left me with Aunt Enid and Uncle Nate when they went to New York for my father's postgraduate work in surgery. David and I were eight years old, going on nine, and we spent a lot of time with Olga.

On Saturdays, Olga polished the hardwood floors and Aunt Enid went downtown with Uncle Nate to have her hair done. As soon as the door closed behind them, Olga turned into a high-spirited war horse. She unpinned the crown of thick blonde braids on her head for reins, David straddled her back in an awkward squat so his full weight wasn't on her, then Olga bucked and shied and cried out warnings of danger.

"Cossacks! Cossacks!" Olga whinnied, tossing her head as she pawed Johnson's paste wax out of the tin and spread it around on the oak battlefield.

"Rat-ta-ta-tat!" David yelled, letting go of Olga's braids to fire his invisible machine gun. "Slash! Slash!" he shouted, swinging his pretend-sword to decapitate more Cossacks. "Got 'em all. Hordes of them. Thanks, old girl." He patted Olga's neck, gave her a smack on the rump, and she backed up to apply more wax. "Watch out for rolling heads, old girl," David yelled. "They're all over the path."

I sat on the roll of Oriental carpet outside the archway to the dining room and just watched at first. There was a lot of whinnying and snorting, shooting and slashing, neighing and yelling. Peace and quiet and good manners didn't seem to matter when Aunt Enid and Uncle Nate were out. I cheered and clapped when David and Olga won all their battles. I laughed at the funny way David had to walk as he rode his faithful horse.

Before they fought their way through the living room, I was invited to ride sidesaddle in front of Prince Charming, as Olga called David. I was a beautiful young princess being rescued from a fate worse than death, Olga said. I didn't believe there was such a thing as a fate worse than death and Olga wouldn't explain what she meant.

A beautiful princess was what I became every Saturday morning until March, when Aunt Enid complained about a disgraceful wax build-up on her lovely floors. David and I had to go with her and sit in Murphy's Beauty Parlour with nothing to do so we wouldn't get in Olga's way while she stripped the floors and started over.

Spring kept coming and going that year, a day of melting and dripping was followed by a week of ice and blizzards. I was afraid summer and my parents would never come back. That was when the long Sunday dinners seemed to stretch on forever.

"No dessert until everybody's plate is clean as a whistle," Uncle Nate said. His eyes were on my plate, as usual. The tiny rose blossoms on

Aunt Enid's Limoges china were hidden under the limp stalks of asparagus I'd spread around.

"It's most impolite for a house guest to leave a single morsel, dear." Aunt Enid put the flat of her hand on the top of the silver bell's stem to indicate she wasn't going to ring it. Olga wasn't going to be able to pretend she heard its tinkle and rush in to clear our plates.

"If she's a guest and not a prisoner, she oughtta be able to leave stuff she hates," David said.

Aunt Enid prided herself on her patience, she often said so while I was there. She could stiffen up and wait an eternity for what she considered mannerly behaviour. "Prisoners are not served asparagus, David. It's a delicacy fit for royalty."

"Quite right," Uncle Nate said. "Emperors, pharaohs, kaisers and kings have all marked spring with feasts of succulent sparrow grass. It can cure bee stings and toothaches as well as taste so delicious you'll be begging for more. Just try some."

"She doesn't have a bee sting or a toothache," David said.

"Princess Elizabeth and Princess Margaret Rose would be delighted if they were served fresh asparagus so early in the season," Aunt Enid said. "They simply adore it." She kept the palm of her hand pressed down on the stem of the silver bell and its rim cut deeper into the table cloth and the silence mat. I waited for the tip of the bell's stem to pop up in the middle of the freckles and veins on the back of her hand. There would be blood everywhere. The table would have to be cleared immediately.

"Bet the princesses don't have to eat what they hate," David said. "Let's pretend she's a princess and can leave whatever she wants."

"*May* leave," Aunt Enid said, "but *she* may *not*."

Uncle Nate did his finger exercises at either side of his empty plate. He was allowed to fidget like that because he had to keep his hands supple for surgery. Olga had to give him a manicure once a week and keep freshly laundered gardening gloves handy for him to wear to his greenhouse. Under the cotton gloves, he wore pink rubber gloves he brought home from the hospital. Olga had to sprinkle the inside of them with cornstarch and hold them open for him so he could slide his hands in without straining a finger. And Uncle Nate was always slathering his hands with Noxzema. I hated the smell. He finished his knuckle-bends before he spoke.

"Their Highnesses, the Princesses, would dearly love to have an uncle like me instead of one who idles away his time with an American divorcee at an unending round of parties. I'm far too busy growing prize gladioli and crowns of asparagus for your pleasure. The princesses would give their eyeteeth for one of those tender spears you won't eat."

I stared at the squashed green caterpillars on my plate and held my breath. The princesses could keep their horsey teeth and have all of the soggy things for all I cared. I would be glad to swallow gladioli leaves, like swords, instead. I would give *my* eyeteeth for the chance.

David waved at the centrepiece, "Why don't you make her eat the flowers? Bet she'd rather. Give her a choice, why don't you?"

He would have sneaked my asparagus into the pockets of his breeches again if he had still been sitting beside me and not across a sea of white linen. But his place at the table had been moved because Uncle Nate caught us burying my asparagus in his greenhouse after the last time it was served.

"Aw, come on, Mother-dear. Ring for good old Olga. She'll wrap up the asparagus and mail it to Buckingham Palace. Nothing's gonna be wasted. Maybe the princesses haven't tasted any since the war started."

Aunt Enid was famous in her church circle, the hospital auxiliary and the IODE for her fancy desserts. We always tested one of her specialties on Sundays. Once she'd even made my favourite lemon sponge pie from the secret recipe my mother left with her. But I sat still, hands folded on my lap, my knife and fork lying across my plate at the correct slant to show I'd finished eating my main course. It wouldn't make David mad at me if we were sent to our rooms to teach us proper manners. We'd get dessert later. Olga always brought us her serving after she'd done the dishes.

Olga had been with Aunt Enid and Uncle Nate since before David was born, long enough to know how to bend their strict rules. Every night except Thursdays, when she had the afternoon and evening off, Olga and David crept into my room after bedtime and she told us stories with gruesome endings. Pauline played with matches and burned herself and her two pet cats to cinders, Albert was a glutton who ate so much he split in half like a melon and had to be buried in two coffins, Boris was such a vicious bully the villagers beat him to death with sticks and fed him to a pack of wild dogs.

"What you expect?" Olga said at the end of them. "Not all children's stories got happy endings."

"Weren't there any kids like us in the Old Country?" I asked one night. "Ones like David and me?"

Olga looked at David and nodded. There was a boy in the village named Ulrich, she said, David was going to look just like him when he grew up. So strong, so handsome, so brave Ulrich was, all the girls in the village loved him. But he had only one sweetheart. She was his cousin. They had promised themselves to each other in secret when they were only small children.

I smiled at David and snuggled down to listen.

Children in the village she came from had many brothers and sisters and cousins, Olga told us, not like David and me. The "good room" of the houses they lived in had a softwood floor that never needed polishing and a tiled fireplace for heat and cooking. The school they went to was in the centre of the village, not out on the prairie like ours, and beside it was the church with its bell tower rising above the rooftops. The priest rang the bell on Sundays, holy days, before weddings and funerals, and he was supposed to ring it to warn the villagers of danger. He was an old, old man, Olga said, deaf to whispered confessions, and that was good, but deaf to the sound of horses' hooves too, and that was bad. His eyes were too marbled by age to see that the torches held high against the dark night sky weren't stars. That night Ulrich and his sweetheart had fallen asleep in their secret meeting place. When the soldiers came there after burning the villagers out of their houses and murdering them, Ulrich ran out of the cow shed with only a pitchfork to protect his sweetheart from a fate worse than death. She saw the soldiers ride him down on their horses. She heard his screams when they used their long knives to cut him as she fled into the forest.

Olga made the sign of the cross on the bib of her apron and was silent.

I sat up. "And then what happened?" I asked. "Did Ulrich get away from the soldiers?"

"Nein." Olga wiped her eyes and hugged David.

"I don't believe it," I said.

"Is truth," Olga said. *"Lügen haben kurze Beine."*

"What's that mean?" David asked.

"Lies have short wings," she said.

"Everyone always dies in your stories and I hate them," I said. "What have they got to do with us? Why should we care if there wasn't enough left of Ulrich to bury?"

But I wanted Olga to tell us that the horses' hooves had flown over Ulrich like feathers, that his knife wounds were healed by a magic moss his sweetheart found in the forest, that they had escaped across the ocean to a place like Regina where soldiers only marched in parades. And I wanted David and Olga to stay in my bedroom with me every night until I could go home.

"Aw, come on, Olga. Be a pal. Tell us a happy story, why don't you? What about when Ulrich's baby boy was born in the New World? She hasn't heard that part. She's gonna have awful nightmares if you don't tell her something good." David patted Olga's back and kept coaxing. "Girls like weddings and stuff."

That's when Olga told us she was going to marry a hospital orderly who lived in Calgary and we could come and visit them often. She said it was all arranged, and hugged David some more. The man's wife had died in childbirth and he needed someone to look after his children. "The *kinder*, that is good," she said. "But the poppa is fat like an elephant and *fünfundfünfzig*!"

"And what?" David asked, nudging me and smirking.

"Fünfundfünfzig!" Olga said.

We laughed. Olga's lips stuck out when she said it and it sounded rude, like one of the long juicy farts Greasy Greer made in the faces of little kids like us at school.

"What's it mean?" I asked.

"Old," Olga said. "The poppa is two times and five how old as me."

"Say it again," David said.

"Fünfundfünfzig! Fünfundfünfzig!" we repeated after her. We said it over and over until we were all laughing so hard we couldn't talk. Olga taught us to take a deep breath before we said it so it would burst out like an explosion. Afterwards, we said it to each other whenever Greasy Greer pushed by us at school, and, if someone did something silly in our Grade 4 classroom, we looked at each other, stuck our lips out, and mouthed it. We even said it very softly behind Aunt Enid's back after she scolded us for having bad manners.

It shocked me to hear Olga say it to Aunt Enid's face. I'd started down to the kitchen for a drink of water and stopped on the landing when I heard Olga saying it. "Fünfundfünfzig! — Fünfundfünfzig?" It didn't sound like she was making a joke.

"He's a prince," Uncle Nate said.

"Olga!" Aunt Enid said. "You'll have his four sons right away. And fifty-five is not too old for a man to give you some more babies of your own. Think of it that way."

"Most Old Country girls would give their eyeteeth for a good man like I've found for you," Uncle Nate said. "He has a clean steady job and he won't be called up and sent overseas to fight *because* of his age."

"And his four motherless sons are the icing on the cake," Aunt Enid said.

"What you expect? I forget David?"

"Yes!" Aunt Enid said, and then lowered her voice so I couldn't hear why. Aunt Enid could present what she called perfectly sensible reasons for anything she wanted done, I'd learned.

David and I were her special attendants when Olga got married in the church with the onion-dome steeple. Aunt Enid insisted on dressing us in kilts and black velvet vests left over from her childhood. We looked just like royalty, she said, and made us put sealer rings around the top of our matching plaid knee socks so they wouldn't droop. Olga was a beautiful bride. Her dress was pale pink instead of white, and she wore a hat instead of a veil, but her unbraided hair fell to her waist like spun gold from a castle tower, I thought. And her fünfundfünfzig elephant wasn't as old or as fat as David and I had imagined. He was dark and quite handsome, like Uncle Nate, but not as tall.

Uncle Nate gave Olga away. During one long part of the ceremony, David and I had to follow the bridal couple around and around an altar. Olga stopped several times and turned around to smooth invisible strands of David's blond hair off his forehead. We held hands and walked ever so carefully: left, right, left, right. We weren't supposed to squish our patent leather shoes and make cracks in them. Aunt Enid had told us, and told us again, she wasn't having Olga put Vaseline on our new shoes every day for weeks just for the good of her health. And she had given us plenty of warnings about the correct way to walk: without looking down at our feet, smiling and smiling, and without any grinning or giggling or being rude in any way whatsoever in a foreign church.

It was the middle of May before I was home again with my own parents — safe and sound and stiff with proper manners. We lived just down the street from David, but I felt as if I'd sailed across the ocean to a new world. We sat on the floor in front of the fireplace and cooked our own hotdogs for dinner the first Sunday. Dessert was as many marshmallows as we wanted to toast.

By the time I was spearing my third marshmallow on the wire clothes hanger, I wasn't feeling as shy anymore. "Aunt Enid and Uncle Nate are awfully old-fashioned," I said.

"Maybe. A little, I guess," my father said.

Mother poked him. "Enid is more than maybe-a-little and Nate is just slightly less than very. Let's be honest."

"Nothing the matter with being old-fashioned about some things." My father lifted my mother's hand to his lips and kissed it, then he did the same to mine. "On the other hand, put a head nurse and a top surgeon together, a stern Scot and a formal German, and you don't get to loll around stuffing marshmallows in your mouth very often."

"Not ever," I said. "They're too old, don't you think? And they don't even look like they're related to you or mom."

My mother gave me a kiss and my father smiled at me. "They're not," he said. "Not all that old and not really related."

"But they're my aunt and uncle," I said.

"Adopted relatives, not blood ones. Your Uncle Nate helped pay my way through medical school and for your mother and me to go to New York so I could study under an old friend of his. Our grandparents came over from the same German colony in Galicia a long time ago. So we're family, in a way. Now he's going to take me into his practice with him."

"But David's my cousin."

"Kissing cousin," my father said.

I blushed, and blew on my marshmallow to put the flame out.

"David is such a handsome boy," Mother said. "And a real Prince Charming, don't you agree?"

I did, and nodded my head because my mouth was full of hot marshmallow. It was true. David was the handsomest boy on our street, in our school, in the entire Queen City. All the girls thought so — especially that show-off Janet Greer. He was popular with the boys because he was so good at sports. He was always picked first for teams. Adults said he was just a born athlete. At the winter competitions in front of the Legislative Building, he won ribbons in snowshoeing and speed skating, and the silver cup for the dog-sled race that had his name and Sir Juggs's engraved on it. Sir Juggs was the old springer spaniel from next door that nobody thought David could train to pull a sled. Our teacher liked David because he was so smart it didn't matter if he fooled around a bit in the classroom. He always stood at the top of our class. Aunt Enid and Uncle Nate were really proud of David's school marks, you could tell by the fuss they made over his report cards. But they never boasted about him. It was bad manners to brag about yourself or a close relative, Aunt Enid said. Maybe she would have been rude enough to do it, though, if she'd heard what Mr. Greer said.

"That Kaufmann kid's a true kraut," he said once at the outdoor rink. "It's Herr Dok-tor's strict German discipline. He's got that master race attitude our boys'll knock out of the squareheads overseas."

Fünfundfünfzig, I thought, sour grapes because all his son could do was fart. What did it matter what he thought?

And then the fight happened.

I didn't warn David.

It all seemed so innocent at first — David passing his love note for Janet Greer across to me, me passing it ahead to her, smiling and smiling as I did it, knowing how obnoxious she would be about adding my cousin to her string of boyfriends. I saw Tommy watching her read the note. Everybody knew he considered himself Janet's boyfriend. He clenched and unclenched his fists, tucking his thumbs under his fingers, springing them out again. But he was David's friend. And all he did after school was run straight home to practise his piano lessons. He lived across the back lane from David and he was getting ready to take his Grade 6 in piano. Sometimes David went over to listen to him play and then stayed for supper and a game of checkers afterwards.

Janet flaunted her note in the cloak room. There was a lot of giggling over it. David had written: *You are the prettiest girl in our room. I'll hit a home run for you after school. Love, D.K.*

We spilled out of the girls' door behind Janet. She led the way across the school yard to the boys' baseball diamonds out on the field. She swished the skirt of her princess-line dress, squealing like a fingernail drawn down a blackboard about how all the boys in Grade 4 liked her best, holding the note up like a conqueror's flag.

The Grade 8 girls ahead of us turned around. "Don't tell me you little kids have a dirty note," one of them said, and reached out for the paper Janet was waving.

Janet gave a shrill cry and crumpled the note against her chest. Before the sound died, Greasy loomed up in front of her, surrounded by his disciples. "You got something to hide?" he snarled. "Hand it over."

I could see David hitting fly balls to warm up, and Tommy behind him, watching.

Greasy Greer belched. Big, fat and stupid, repeating his Grade 8 for the second time. He was always bragging about how he was going to join up and wipe out the Nazi pigs. He wouldn't have had to lie about his age to join the army. "You get a dirty note from one of them little pricks in your room?" He grabbed Janet's wrist and twisted it.

Janet stood on tiptoe and said something in his ear.

"Kaufmann? That little Hun?" Greasy said. He grabbed the note, held it up over his head, and tore it into tiny pieces, letting the bits fall on his brushcut like dandruff. More belches rumbled up from his stomach as he did it, then he farted. "That's what a Canuck does to a Nazi!" he said. "Shred 'em to shit so's they can't say dirty words in German at ya when ya pass 'em."

"David! Watch out!" I tried to get through the crowd to him. The Grade 8 girls grabbed me. I was starting to cry. "Let go," I screamed. "Let me go or I'm telling." I saw Tommy tackle David. They were on the ground wrestling. Greasy Greer reached into the tangle, grabbed up the bat. The other big boys yanked David and Tommy up, tore them apart.

"Hang onto that Heinie!" Greasy slammed the bat on the ground, spat on it, pressed Tommy's hands around the handle, his big meaty hands over them. "Wanna fight the Nazi scum? Don't bust your *piana* hands." Greasy's hands were wrapped tighter than butcher's paper around Tommy's. He swung the bat. It hit David in the face. There was an awful sound, like a boot smashing through rubber ice.

Cheers. Taunts. Screaming and screaming and screaming. "Stop! Oh, stop! Let my cousin go. I'm telling, I'm telling, I'm telling!" David's hands were gone. They'd wrapped them around his back. Big, plaid-shirted boys holding him — hiding behind him. "Hit the Hun! Swing harder! I got your hands protected, Piana-prick." Whirling, whirling. Blood and thuds and cries for mercy.

Tommy was sobbing, choking, trying to yank his hands free from under Greasy's, but the bat kept swinging back and forth, thudding against David's body like the thump of my heart.

It didn't stop until David was unconscious, broken and bleeding, lying crumpled on the Grade 4 Lilac School baseball diamond like an empty gym bag.

Too late, I twisted my arms from the grips of the big girls and ran howling for help.

The fight became a secret, something to be ashamed of, something to be hidden from the polite and patriotic people concerned with the horrors of the war in Europe. They weren't told that David swallowed three baby teeth and lost a permanent tooth on the Grade 4 baseball diamond. The police weren't involved; the big boys weren't punished; Greasy Greer didn't answer any questions. Ours was a good neighbourhood of fine Anglo-Saxon families, except for us. Hoodlums were not bred there. And a victim in the family is not something to discuss with others. We knew how to keep it quiet. Doctors and their families know how to keep dark secrets.

Against Aunt Enid's and Uncle Nate's wishes, my father took me to see David in the hospital a week after the fight. He was bandages, casts, straps and pulleys. His eyes were red slits in soft hills of blue-green flesh. There was a sharp smell of Noxzema and rotten potatoes in the room. My stomach heaved. I held my breath.

There wasn't anywhere to kiss his face that didn't look too tender to touch with a feather. I sat and stroked one of his hands, like my father was doing. David couldn't speak. His jaw was wired shut, his lips swollen and split. I didn't know what to say, what else to do. But if I looked at his hands, only his hands, I was able to believe there hadn't been any fight at all. He was alive. Recovering. He would get better.

But he didn't get better. He got worse. He had to drop out of school. The seizures he started to have in the hospital became more frequent and violent. Nobody at school asked about him, not even our teacher. Aunt Enid and Uncle Nate finally took him to a specialist in Montreal.

"Severe chronic idiopathic epilepsy," Uncle Nate told my father when they got back.

My father groaned. "Can't he do better than that with his training and special equipment?"

"Refused to commit himself to stating a cause. He speculated the *incident* at school was triggered by David's first grand mal seizure. Said that would account for the big boys having to hold him down with enough force to break bones and tear muscles."

"Christ!" My father hit the palm of his hand with his fist. "That's god-damned bloody nonsense. There were witnesses."

Uncle Nate's hands dangled like dead fish at his sides. "He looks like the same handsome little boy, doesn't he? But he won't for long if we can't stop the seizures. And surgery isn't an option."

My father put his arm around Uncle Nate's shoulders and they just stood there, looking out our living room window.

David's condition was never discussed in my hearing again. The fall I started high school, Aunt Enid and Uncle Nate legally changed their last name from Kaufmann to Cameron, Aunt Enid's maiden name. They sent David away to a "school" in Alberta and shortly after they moved to Edmonton themselves to be closer to him. Our *family* ties loosened. We got the bad news that Aunt Enid and Uncle Nate were killed in a head-on collision with an army transport truck on their way to visit David. I was married by then and had two girls and two boys. I was busy doing my best to prove that Olga was wrong when she said not all children's stories had happy endings.

I thought of David right away when I heard that my husband's family reunion was going to be held in Red Deer, Alberta. David had sent me a length of Cameron tartan from Red Deer back around 1951. It had a professionally printed card on it to say he had handwoven it. I must have written a thank-you note to him. I must have. But that was our last contact.

My husband belongs to a huge family with relatives all over the West. They're always discovering another cousin or in-law to cement into the family circle. In the midst of the "Love Em And Squeeze Em Welcome Reception", while everybody was hugging and kissing and toasting funny things they remembered about each other, I slipped away and went to the sprawling brick institution. I asked for David under both names, Kaufmann and Cameron. Transferred to Colonel Belcher's in Calgary, they said, after making a long search through their records. It had happened a long time ago. No one in the office remembered him.

My husband agreed to stop in Calgary on the way home, which it really wasn't. I called Colonel Belcher's as soon as we got a motel room. "Yes-yes," the woman who answered the telephone said. "He *is* a patient here. He'll be so glad to see a relative, at last. He never gets any visitors."

The wild-looking young man who grabbed me in a bear hug at the reception desk wasn't my cousin. He was an Indian. He hung onto me and shouted obscenities at the orderly who was trying to explain it was David Cameron I was looking for, not Cameron David. He didn't care about the order of his name, he said, I could call him anything I liked. He kept pulling me back when I tried to leave, calling me his little sister, yelling about the fire on the reserve that I had to remember because I was there with him when it happened.

I found David in a new institute across town; in the bright yellow wing — the chronic intensive care unit, according to the "You Are Here" map on the wall. The place seemed to be empty of staff and patients. A young girl strapped into a wheelchair was sitting inside a linen room, stabbing her hands at shelves of marigold towels and bedding. After a frustrating pantomime, I finally figured out what she wanted. I tugged a towel and washcloth down off the top shelf and tucked them under the straps across her lap. She smiled and smiled. I asked if she knew which room was David Cameron's. She spun her chair around and led me to a door. She left me there. The door was closed.

I moved back. Turned away. Walked the primary-coloured halls until I found a woman in uniform.

"Excuse me," I said. "I've come to visit David Cameron. Room 105? The door is closed and I wondered —"

"Oh, he's in there all right," she said. "Can't take him out of his room, Sunday or not. Takes fits like a machine gun, poor old guy."

"Fits?" I said. "You mean epileptic seizures?"

"Can't even strap him into a chair, he's so bad. Been known to tip them right over and get in an awful mess. Did it one place he was in and landed against a hot rad. Thrashed himself against it real bad before someone found him."

"But I can see him?" I asked. "Just walk in? Should I knock?"

"Not if you expect him to answer. Wonder the poor thing's not dead. Worse than being a vegetable, fits like he has. Some of the staff's afraid to go near him. His mom used to cope with them real good when she came visiting, before she moved."

"His mom?" I asked. Aunt Enid had been dead for years.

"Too bad for old Dave she moved to the Okanagan. Kelowna, I think she said she was going, to be with her other sons. You from one of the church groups?"

"I'm his cousin," I said. "His mom. My aunt. We've lost touch."

"An angel in our books, ask any of the staff, way she took over for us when she came. Even had a halo, we used to tell her, silver braids wound up there on top of her head."

It's a large single room, a misshapen triangle, the side walls joined in a V. There's a narrow, ceiling-to-floor, sealed window at one side of the point where the walls meet. It lets a slice of outside light into the room, but there isn't enough floor space in that corner to put a wheelchair.

The bright yellow walls are bare, except for one of those plastic-framed mats that have different shaped slots in them to display family snapshots. But the photographs of professional models are still in it. Where are David and Sir Juggs with their silver cup? Where are David and I blowing out the candles on his ninth birthday cake, Olga standing behind us looking so proud? Strangers look down on him, keep him company: smiling and smiling; hands, gently touching hands, resting on a strong shoulder, holding a white Bible with cream-coloured orchids on it. There are pictures of fresh-cut flowers in a silver bowl, picnic-green grass, long willow leaves brushing dimples in a shiny blue stream, and children playing.

He is asleep, or unconscious, in a king-sized crib that has padded sides. Part of his limbs are encased in plaster. His right arm and left leg lie bent, like wishbone halves, on top of the yellow thermal blanket. And his face. Oh, his face. His forehead bulges and plunges. His nose is flattened to wet holes. Bubbles of blood-flecked spittle lie on gnawed lips. His chin is a stubbled bruised hump slashed with stitched crevices. His wasted muscles keep twitching and jerking. But his eyes are closed, eyelids sunk deep in his skull as if they had pennies pressed on them.

There is nothing to say. Nothing to do.

There is no use praying to a Saviour who said, "Suffer little children to come unto me."

Olga knows that David is one of those children whose story does not have a happy ending. And I know what Aunt Enid and Uncle Nate saw when they closed their eyes and gazed blindly upwards: David lying still, tall baskets of gladioli beside his coffin, their leaves crossed like swords over him.

I kiss his cheek lightly. It takes all of my courage. I want him to die. I want to kill him.

Just a pillow, pressed softly on his face, held there, until his fight is won.

Star Bright

Vickie is waiting for Keith in the listening room. The talking dolls tape is set up on the reel-to-reel Sony ready for him to hear. As usual, Keith is late.

"*Vickie loves Keith & Keith loves Vickie,*" Vickie scribbles on the notes she made for splicing the dialogue of GI Joe and Best Friend Cynthia together.

She puts the red marking pencil in her mouth and inhales. Listening to Best Friend Cynthia has left her feeling spinny, as giddy as a girl in love for the first time. Too bad it isn't that simple, she thinks, she wishes it was. She wishes she had a cigarette to help her think clearly about true love and her media career. She takes the pencil out of her mouth and exhales.

Vickie Ann Seitz, she asks herself, what do you need to be happy, happy?

She draws two stars, prints her name in one, Keith's in the other, connects them with lightning bolts, and sketches a television screen around them.

Smack on focus, she thinks, teamwork with Keith is helping her use radio as a launch pad to stardom on TV. That's what she needs to be happy. John is not in the picture.

How to tell John she wants a divorce has been worrying her thin for weeks. In fact, she has lost fifteen pounds — which is five pounds more than the television cameras add on, and that's great. What she has to do now, tonight, is level with John, get it over with, and not put an ounce of that weight back on again after he's gone out of her life.

Poor John is going to be devastated, she knows it. He still seems to think he can mould her into a replica of her mother, into a sweetness-and-light happy housewife, a household goddess. Lately, he has been offering her boxes of Hostess chips and Belgian chocolates to try and woo her away from her scripts for midnight munchies, and then a little love-making in the master bedroom. Eating in bed just isn't John's thing. John is the kind of man who perches on his side of the bed each night to rub the soles of his bare feet together in case there's any lint on them that might come off in the sheets. She used to think it was cute and sort of sexy, like watching a frog-prince balance on the edge of his ladylove's lilypad to perform a mating dance. Once upon a time it really turned her on.

Not anymore. Not since Keith came on the scene as the new announcer-producer of the radio program that uses her freelance items. Behind the urban cowboy facade Keith adopted to move west from Winnipeg, there's a seasoned media type she can really relate to. As a workmate, Keith has taught her a lot. And as a playmate, he's a boots-on-the-bedspread kind of guy. She smiles.

Keith happens to be staying in the Embassy Hotel's newly renovated bridal suite, one of the few rooms the hotel has with a private bathroom, and he claims the fake fur bedspread is one hundred per cent virgin acrylic mink. It covers an under-filled waterbed that would make anyone except lovers on tight deadlines seasick. Nine mirror tiles are on the ceiling over the waterbed and a black velvet painting hangs on the red and gold flocked wallpaper at the foot of it. The painting is of a naked couple, artfully entwined so none of their sexual parts show. They're standing in the beam of a full orange moon under a fluorescent green palm tree that has its fronds dangling down around their hot pink flesh like snakes. Keith calls the painting, "Mr. and Mrs. Canuck Stuck Standing-up In Hawaii". Compared to the Wedgwood blue chintz, white walls and watercolour prints of what she'll soon be able to call the "Ms." bedroom at home, it's like travelling to another continent to follow Keith down the street from the radio station to the bridal suite.

Vickie is doodling hearts and flowers when Keith sneaks up behind her and kisses the bump of knowledge on the back of her head.

"Oh! At last!" she says, quickly turning her notes over.

"Apologies, Pardner," Keith growls in the Ben Cartwright voice that makes girls and women write the station for his autographed picture. "Didn't mean to keep the best brains in broadcasting hitched to the listening post this long. Got problems?"

"Nothing I couldn't handle," Vickie says. "GI Joe's voice sounded like grinding gears when I recorded it, but I got Super Tech to filter it. He hasn't been programmed to say much, anyway. I kept pulling his dog tag to see if I'd missed anything, but I hadn't. Best Friend Cynthia's a real chatterbox, of course. Talk about sexist stereotyping! Did I tell you her records are even labelled by topic? 'Get Acquainted' and 'Family' on the flip sides of one disc, 'Outdoor' and 'Indoor' topics on the other one?''

"Yup," Keith says.

"And what little girls have to do to make her talk?"

Keith says, "Nope."

"They have to hike up her dress, pull down her panties, stick a disc into the slot in her stomach, and then press down hard on it, practically make a fist and punch her in the stomach, every time they want the doll to say something. I wish we were doing this for television so my audience could see me expose *that*."

"Radio-vision's what we're after here. Send the sound of a breaking nose out on the airwaves, smack on focus, and folks'll see the fist hit, the bone break, the blood spill. How many times have I chewed that cud of wisdom over with you, Pardner?"

Too many, Vickie thinks, and one of the first things she's going to change about Keith is his phony cowpoke jargon.

"How long's the tape?" Keith helps himself to the stopwatch she has hanging around her neck on a black cord.

It's matter of fact, he doesn't fondle, but dammit, her nipples stand at attention anyway. And she can smell the chocolate scented pipe tobacco Keith uses. Why didn't *he* take the pledge at the Seventh Day Adventist Stop Smoking Clinic at the City Health Centre and report *his* experience trying to quit on-air?

"In Turkey in 1605," Vickie says, "anyone caught smoking a pipe had his nose pierced with its stem and was put on public exhibit. If that didn't stop him, the sultan's death penalty for second offenses was a sure cure, the ultimate cold turkey: he was beheaded."

Keith pats her head. "Tough assignment, eh, Pardner?"

"Listening to B.F. Cindy all those hours without a cigarette? It freaked me out. Gave me a stomach-ache. I almost threw up all over the tape machine listening to her silly chatter without any nicotine to settle my nerves. I haven't done the final timing. It's about one and a half minutes, I think. I was making notes on how to introduce the item and waiting for you to get here so I'd only have to listen to her once more today, not twice."

"Here I am, Pardner." Keith clicks her stopwatch on, off, and resets it at 60. "Roll the tape."

Vickie turns the switch of the tape machine to the forward arrow and, thanks to her work with a one-sided razor blade and splicing tape

— skills Keith taught her — the voices of talking dolls GI Joe and Best Friend Cynthia fill the listening room:

I've got a tough assignment for you.

You and I are a lot alike, isn't that groovy?
Do you wear much makeup? I like the natural
look, don't you? Why don't we call your
friends? I'd love to meet them.

This is going to be rough.

I've always wanted to be a doctor or nurse
because I like to help sick people feel better.
Let's listen to some music. Play your favourite
record.

Can you handle it?

I love popcorn. Can we make some? No more
French fries or milkshakes for me for awhile.
I gained two pounds last weekend. What's
your favourite sport?

Follow me.

I'm glad you're my best friend and I can tell
you all my secrets. Will you tell me a secret?

Follow me. We must get there before dark.

Will you vote for me for class president?
Will you help me bake cookies for the bake sale?
Let's exchange phone numbers and you can call
me tonight.

The Adventure Team is needed in Africa.

I can't wait until we're old enough to travel
together. Do you have any pictures of places
you'd like to visit? Don't forget to bring
your camera with us today.

Follow me. Can you handle it?

I really love my family. Do you want to go
horseback riding? Last time I rode the most
beautiful palomino.

This is going to be rough.

I'm glad we're so close. I've always wanted
my very own horse, haven't you?

Mission accomplished. Good work, men.

Vickie presses Keith's thumb down on the stopwatch.

"One thirty-eight," he says. "Cut 'doctor' and you've got it smack on focus." He bunts her nose with his knuckles. "Gotta hit the trail to do voice-overs on some TV commercials. See you at the Embassy after your Dear John act, Pardner." He hangs the stopwatch around her neck and he's gone.

Vickie waits until the pressure mechanism on the listening room door has sucked it shut. Then she backs up the tape, finds "doctor or . . .", marks it to cut so Best Friend Cynthia will only say she wants to be a nurse, picks up the razor blade, and changes her mind. It stays. She thinks she knows why it's there. A feminist actress in need of money recorded Best Friend Cynthia's voice and managed to slip "doctor" into the script she had to follow so that little girls could squeeze at least one small liberated thought out of their talking doll's gut.

She rewinds the tape, puts it in the box, and labels it: *Talking Dolls Xmas Feature*; Time: 1:38; Opening Cue: "I've got a tough. . ." Closing Cue: ". . .men."

Men! Sometimes she wonders if they're worth all the hassle. She stuffs the tape into her briefcase, which she uses as her purse, cosmetic kit and research file. In it, she has various shades of blush and mascara and moisture-proof lipsticks, FDS and her birth control pills in their wheel-of-fortune dispenser; plus pamphlets and articles and notes on VD symptoms, adult bedwetting cures, a new drug abuse program, instructions on how to knit a uterus (part of a kit for teachers of natural childbirth in rural areas), a booklet on how to obtain a quickie do-it-yourself divorce for a maximum lawyer's fee of seventy-five dollars, and her historical facts about smoking. But there aren't any cigarettes in it. Not even a squashed one at the bottom. Nothing to reward herself for finally getting the damn talking dolls recorded and spliced together in dialogue on one tape. Nothing to relieve her trembly craving so she can think straight and plan a script for breaking the news to John tonight. No, she has to resort to repeating bits of anti-smoking history to herself again.

Vickie leaves the radio station saying to herself: A Russian czar, tah-dah tah-dah, one of the first public health pioneers, had smokers brutally beaten, then banished them to Siberia.

It doesn't dull her craving or make her glad she only has to use will power, but she has an idea. What if she got started on the quickie divorce right away? — like tomorrow? She could quit the damn Stop

Smoking Clinic and use her experience ending her marriage to do a new series of "Spotlight On Life" features. Maybe, after he was over the initial shock, John would let her interview him to balance it with a male viewpoint? Why not? She'll talk him into it. And broadcasting her modern divorce would probably increase her ratings on Keith's program. She could lead into each feature with a detail from her old-fashioned wedding to give the series that cigarette ad ambience of *You've come a long way, Baby.*

Three years ago on Boxing Day, she thought being a bride was the only starring role she would ever want.

It was a beautiful, beautiful, traditional marriage ceremony. A High Mass. A choir to sing "The Lord's Prayer" instead of the Christian Folk Singers doing "This Is Love", an organ instead of guitars. Rice, not confetti, given to the guests by the ushers to shower on them as they left the cathedral. Instead of fake silk flowers, there were bushels and bushels of fresh flowers everywhere; in the bouquets, boutonnieres and corsages, banked on the altar and around the bride's table on the stage of the hotel ballroom, in arrangements at the centre of all the round dinner tables. Five hundred guests had toasted her with champagne. Her mother wept. So did her father, although he tried to pretend his tears were because of what it was costing.

There will be tears when she tells her parents about the divorce, too, she knows it. And what if she had let her parents talk her into taking the money and eloping, like they did? John was all for it. She can thank her lucky stars she wasn't. She wouldn't have such a perfect dramatic contrast to a seventy-five-dollar divorce to use on air. She'll have to tell her parents that. But what was it her mother said when she asked her if she'd ever wanted to divorce her father? — "Divorce? Never. Murder, maybe." — and then her parents looked at each other in that secret way they had of communicating that left her totally out. Well, this isn't the era of love and marriage hitched together like a horse and carriage that her parents sing duets about. These days, she'll remind them, you *can* have one without the other, and lots of career women do.

Vickie isn't surprised to find a parking ticket under the windshield wiper of John's car. She'd parked it in front of the Embassy so long ago there could have been half a dozen tickets there. Poor John, she thinks, recalling how eagerly he'd offered her his car keys when her car wouldn't start. In return for him taking the bus, she'd promised to whip right home from the Stop Smoking Clinic and prepare him a special home-cooked dinner, have candlelight and wine, just for the two of them, like she used to do when they were first married and she wasn't freelancing. They would have a heart-to-heart, she'd told him. Actually, Vickie has ordered the divorce dinner from Homestyle Caterers on Dewdney Avenue and she's going over there to pick it up now. Another career choice John wouldn't understand, and Keith would, she thinks. But she closes the glove compartment and sticks the parking ticket in her briefcase instead. Five dollars if she pays it within seven days. A divorce present. Pay John's parking ticket, she'll add to her list of the things she still has to do before tomorrow's program.

Let's see, Vickie thinks as she wheels the car out of the tight parking space, after John leaves tonight, she'll have to finish the talking dolls script, come up with a snappy introduction for a tape that took that much work, and think of something inspirational about quitting smoking for her finale to that series. She wishes she hadn't already used the story about the woman dying of lung cancer, the one who was so badly addicted she lit her last cigarette in an oxygen tent and burnt to death. She wishes she didn't understand how that poor woman felt. She can't even dig into the ashtray of John's car for a butt. John hasn't smoked since he was eight years old. Back then, he thought the men in town smoked to keep their hands warm, so he and his pal tried smoking dried leaves rolled in newspaper and made themselves sick. Right now, Vickie would settle for manure rolled in toilet paper.

Vickie steps on the gas and says to herself: King James the First of England proclaimed smoking was barbarous, beastly, hateful to the nose, a vile and stinking custom, harmful to the brain.

And she sails through the red light as far as the middle of the intersection before the truck broadsides her.

The impact crushes in the passenger door, pops the empty ashtray out on her lap, and spins John's red Toyota around like a top. As soon as the car comes to a stop, Vickie throws the gear shift into park, hops out, dodges the vehicles careening by her with their horns blaring, and sprints over to the driver's side of the Brown's Auction truck that hit her.

"Oh, I'm so sorry," she says to the ashen-faced driver. "I know it's all my fault for going through a red light but I took the pledge at the Seventh Day Adventist Stop Smoking Clinic at the City Health Centre and I was telling myself what King James the First of England proclaimed to stop my craving for nicotine because I'm telling my husband I want a divorce tonight and the stress makes me sneak puffs of cigarettes whenever I get the chance so I don't know if God got me for that or for cheating on my husband because we had a High Mass when we took our vows and now I'm in love with a cowboy from Winnipeg."

The truck driver's face has turned scarlet. Has she said all that stuff out loud? It feels as if dozens of small fists are punching her in the stomach. "Oh, God," she says. "Have I been babbling worse than Best Friend Cynthia? I just wanted you to know I'm really sorry for going through that red light."

"Hey, lady? Listen, lady, it's okay," the driver says. "As long as you're not hurt. People go through red lights sometimes, eh? Like they just don't see them."

"Oh, but I do, I do," she hears herself say, and wishes she didn't. Her voice sounds squeaky again. She has to pull herself together, quit acting as if she's a talking doll with a record in her stomach. Vickie flops over and does the rag doll exercise to relax herself, lower her voice, like Keith taught her to do before she goes on air. "My profession involves red lights," she says in her radio voice. "They mean I'm in a live studio and —"

"Hey, listen, lady, it's pretty live round here and we're gonna get ourselves killed if we don't get outta the crossfire."

"Please, could you lend me a cigarette?" Vickie asks, hating the whine she can hear has crept back into her voice. She can't stand women who plead with men. "Please?" she says.

"I don't smoke, lady. Listen, why don't you go get into your car, follow me, and we'll go to the cop shop to report this accident, okay? Can you handle that? Follow me," the driver says.

Vickie nods her head. She's afraid if she speaks she'll tell him he sounds like GI Joe. Bits of plastic and glass and red metal make a trail for her to follow back to John's car. She stops to pick up the chrome door handle.

The truck driver leans on his horn and shouts, "Hey, lady? It's okay, eh? That's not your kitchen floor. You don't have to do that. The city's got a crew comes round to clean up. You're gonna get us both creamed."

It's almost five o'clock. Rush hour. And hordes of people are taking advantage of Thursday night store opening to go Christmas shopping. But Vickie follows the Brown's Auction truck as if John's car was being towed behind it on a short chain. The truck driver keeps blinking the brake lights to signal her to fall back, but she doesn't want to lose him. She wants to march into the police station with him, admit she went through a red light, and show him she isn't just some silly housewife who can't stop talking and doesn't know how to drive.

She is pleased that the driver is standing on the sidewalk at the rear of his truck when she swoops back into the parallel parking space behind it that isn't an inch longer than John's car. Vickie slips the car in so tight to the curb he steps back from it.

"Hey, not bad, lady," he says, when she gets out. "Couldn't have slid that crushed tin can of yours into there better myself."

"The car belongs to my husband," Vickie says, and she lets the truck driver open the doors into the police station for her.

The policeman behind the counter she marches right up to is smoking. The fists pound her stomach again. She takes a deep breath and says, "Warning! Health and Welfare Canada advises that danger to health increases with amount smoked — avoid inhaling."

"Chief's Clean Air Committee send you to hassle me?" The policeman carefully stubs out his cigarette and tucks the long butt back in his Rothman's pack. "You one of his nicotine narcs?"

"No, no. I'm just another nicotine addict," Vickie says, and smiles at him. Okay, that's the truth, she tells herself, now get to the point and don't tell him anything else personal — no babbling. "I've followed this nice gentleman here to report an accident that's entirely my fault."

"Hah! Who's gonna walk in here and admit that? What's the catch?" The smell of smoke on the policeman's breath makes Vickie lean over the counter closer to him and breathe deeply.

"No catch," the truck driver says. "Hear the lady out, eh?"

"Well, I was on my way to the caterer's. To pick up a special divorce dinner to serve my husband." Vickie is speaking slowly, trying to inhale more than she exhales. "I had a lot of things on my mind. Talking dolls. Do-it-yourself divorce. The pledge I'd taken at the Seventh Day Adventist Stop Smoking Clinic at the City Health Centre. And, you know how it is. Going cold turkey? It isn't easy under pressure. You need a cigarette."

"Hah!" the policeman says. "Tell me about it."

Vickie smiles. So far, so good. She's enunciating, moving her lips, speaking softly, but clearly. People who ought to be a lot less nervous than she is have just nodded or shaken their heads when she holds a microphone in front of them during street interviews to get their opinion on something. They often ask her if they're going to be on television. She wants to give the policeman radio-vision, let him see the fist hit, the bone break, the blood run.

"Well, I guess I had a nicotine fit. I went through a red light. Or almost through it. This gentleman couldn't avoid hitting me. With his truck. Dead centre in the middle of the intersection. May I borrow a cigarette?"

The policeman takes the pack of Rothman's out of his shirt pocket, opens it, pulls a cigarette half-way out, offers it to her, then re-lights his butt.

"Thank you," Vickie says. She puts the cigarette in the centre of her mouth like a baby's soother. The policeman holds his lighter under it. "No, no, don't light it," she says. "I'll keep it for later, for after I tell my husband I'm in love with an urban cowboy and want a divorce. Do you mind?"

"It's a gift, not a loan, sweetheart," the policeman says. "Now then, let's see your drivers' licences and registrations."

Vickie begins poking through her briefcase.

"No problem," the truck driver says. He pulls his credentials out of the back pocket of his jeans and hands them over. "I didn't even get a dent in the bumper when I hit her, eh? There won't be no government insurance claim from me or Brown's Auctions." The policeman records some numbers and gives the papers back to him.

"Guess you can handle it okay from here, eh, lady?" The truck driver gives her a light punch on the arm before he goes.

"Keep truckin," Vickie says, and dumps the contents of her briefcase out on the counter. "I don't have the registration," she says to the policeman. "I've got poor John's car today. But my driver's licence is in here somewhere. In my wallet, if we can find that."

"Hah! Looks like you got plenty of problems to solve, sweetheart," the policeman says. "Don't touch a drop of coffee after breakfast's the answer to one of them, I learned." He holds up the pamphlet on adult bedwetting. He sifts through some more of her research, shaking his head, then stops with the mimeographed natural childbirth instructions in front of him. "Bert?" he turns and calls. "Come on out here. Need your help. You're not gonna believe this. Your wife can quit crying about the female surgery she got. Just take her a Xerox of these here instructions on how to knit herself a uterus."

An older policeman with white hair comes out to the counter. He reminds Vickie of her father. "Oh, hi," she says. "We're looking for my licence because I went through a red light and got hit by a Brown's Auction truck and I'm hoping you'll have to arrest me so I don't have to go to the Seventh Day Adventist Stop Smoking Clinic at the City Health Centre and then go home without any dinner to tell my husband I want a divorce." It's those fists again, she thinks, God is turning me into Best Friend Cynthia. She sees her lighter in some VD folders and decides to have a few calming puffs of the cigarette. She lights up, takes one long drag, and stubs the cigarette out in the tin ashtray the first policeman takes out from under the counter and shoves toward her.

The policemen find her driver's licence caught in the wheel-of-fortune card that holds her birth control pills. They take it, and the uterus knitting instructions, and disappear with them into the office behind the counter. She lights up again, takes two long drags this time, and lets the cigarette burn in the ashtray. Men, she thinks, where is my one true love? Why am I always waiting on men to come and go in my life, dammit?

"No charges," the first policeman says when they appear again. "Far as we're concerned, we didn't hear no confession about going through no red light or nothing."

Bert, the one who looks like her father, says, "We think you've got enough troubles already, dear. My advice? Keep yourself busy with something constructive, you know? Otherwise, you get a divorce and you're just going to get screwed, know what I mean? Think you can handle driving yourself home to the one-and-only? It's dark and slippery out there. Want us to call a cruiser to take you?"

"Oh, no thank you," Vickie says. "I'm really a very good driver, but that's very kind of you to offer. I'm glad to find out policemen are so friendly, so, uh, understanding and forgiving. Wait until I tell Keith how nice you both were to me. We'll have to do some really upbeat broadcasts about policemen — interviews that show a policeman can be your best friend? — that sort of theme?"

"Will we be on television?" Bert asks, smoothing his hair.

"Radio-vision," Vickie says. "And thanks for the cigarette. I'll finish it after I tell John the news. Merry Christmas!" They both smile at her. They have such nice smiles, she thinks as she hurries to the car.

Her list must be rearranged now. She hasn't got time to go to the Stop Smoking Clinic, pick up the dinner, get wine, candles, or a loaf of French bread to break with John after she tells him what she has decided to do. And, she almost forgot, she was going to stop at her mom and dad's and break the news to them first, tell them she needs their support, warn them not to go babying John when he runs to them begging to know what else he can do to make her happy, tell her parents she doesn't need any lectures about loyalty to her husband and to her marriage vows. They know she has to follow her own star.

Vickie steps on the gas and thinks about the motto she has on the wall over her desk at the radio station: *Whatever women do, they must do twice as well as men. Fortunately, that's not difficult.*

Unfortunately, sometimes it's damn difficult, she thinks, and telling her parents, telling John she doesn't love him anymore — and about his banged-up car — is going to be one of those times. And then she has those scripts to do, the divorce booklet to research, and Keith expecting her to show up at his passion pit in the Embassy. Men! None of them can ever understand what a tough assignment it is for her to splice together a personal life with a meteoric rise to TV stardom. Maybe a woman with her ambition ought to just stop falling in love.

But Venus shines bright in the clear December sky and Vickie makes her old wish. Star light, star bright, Vickie says to herself, wish I may, wish I might, be with the one I love tonight.

The next thing Vickie knows, she's checking in at the Landmark Motel. The contents of her briefcase are strewn along the reception counter, and the clerk, a pleasant looking older woman who recognized her voice from hearing her on the radio, is helping her look for her Visa.

"Now tell me," the woman says, thumbing through the divorce booklet without any luck. "Is Keith as handsome as he sounds?"

"Yes, yes I guess he is," Vickie says. That damn Visa, she thinks, it's got to be in here somewhere.

Vital Statistic

I know ninth birthdays aren't usually that special. You're not one whole decade old. You've still got three years to go before twelve, an even dozen. And being a teenager is so far in the future it's hard to imagine ever being that grown up. But reaching nine years old turned out to be a matter of life or death for me.

Nine wouldn't have been such a significant birthday if it weren't for our dog. He'd been around since before I was born so he was jealous of me. His name was Schultz and he was everybody's best friend — except mine. Nothing I could do, however hard I tried, made him like me.

Schultz was mostly dachshund. My parents said he was a cross between a purebred dachshund and a devious terrier who had ruined his mother's life in show business. With me, he acted as if his father had been a pit bull terrier.

My mother could bath him, brush him, and even spank him when he got up on the table and ate the pickles or cheese, and Schultz would lick her hand. Then he would sit at her feet, looking up at her adoringly, like a stuffed toy with a felt mouth stitched on its face that went up at the corners in a smile.

My father played ball with Schultz on the living room rug and, whenever we had company, showed off how he could sit pretty, roll over, and shake a paw.

Grandma rubbed Schultz's head with her shoe while she sat and drank coffee at the kitchen table, sometimes kicking him when she crossed her legs, but you wouldn't hear a growl. When she shook her

Zoom-A-Long mop — which was about a thousand times a day — he just sat and watched the head flop without trying to catch it and tear it to bits.

Jane, my sister who's four years older than me and has always wanted a horse, taught Schultz to jump over barriers she built that were more than twice as high as he was. He could have jumped over my head, but he wouldn't come near me if he could avoid it, and he didn't want me coming near him. Schultz slept on Jane's bed and kept her feet warm. She told him bedtime stories about squirrels and mice and cute little skunks that would love to play with a sweet little dog like him. But if I approached her bed, holding the back of my hand out and speaking softly, like you're supposed to do with strange dogs, he immediately turned into a snarling dragon.

Everybody, including me, praised Schultz all the time for being able to jump so high, never shedding any hair, and for acting so intelligent. I was the only one he didn't waggle up to afterwards for a pat on the head. I was the only one he never jumped up beside to lick my face. If I offered him a Milk Bone, he turned up his nose at it. When I filled his water bowl, he wouldn't drink from anywhere else but the toilet. If I threw his ball for him, he looked the other way or began chasing his tail. He chewed up my school workbooks, my mitts, my toque, and one of my rubber boots. I almost stopped trying to be friends with him after what he did to my Barbie doll.

I'd saved up my allowance for weeks to buy Barbie a super hot pants outfit in bright pink. It had a matching headband and high-heeled sandals.

"Hey, Jane, look how cool my Barbie doll looks in her new outfit," I said, running out of our bedroom holding Barbie up just by the heels of her new sandals and turning her around in my hand so Jane could get the full effect.

Jane was lying on the chesterfield reading *Black Beauty* for the umpteenth time. Schultz was lying beside her. He growled as I came closer. "Can it, Schultzie," Jane said, tapping him on the snout. "Let me see," she said to me. "Did you pay four ninety-five for that little bit of material?"

I was just going to hand Barbie to her when Schultz jumped up and snapped my doll's head off.

"Schultz!" Jane yelled, and then she started to laugh. He was tossing Barbie's head up in the air and then catching it in his mouth. Her headband slid over her face and, when he caught her head in his mouth, her pony tail hung out of it as if he had a long yellow tongue. "Gross, Schultzie. Oh, that's so gross," Jane kept saying.

I was standing there in shock, the decapitated body of Barbie still twirling in my hand.

I tried to tell my parents that I hadn't been teasing Schultz with Barbie, but they wouldn't believe me.

"Jealousy," my father said, "is a terrible affliction. Just because Jane wouldn't play Barbie dolls with you is no reason to torment a little dog — an old, smart, high-jumping, loving and almost purebred dachshund, I might add."

"Who doesn't shed a hair for your grandmother to mop up and is completely housebroken," my mother threw in.

Holy smoke, I thought. What do you say to that? I mean, sometimes, by accident, I still wet my bed. But if I said that Schultz was jealous of me, my parents probably would have chained *me* up in the back yard and called the pound.

It was a hot summer day when my parents finally saw that I hadn't been lying about Schultz having it in for me, rather than the other way around.

We were on holidays at Lake Katepwa, doing lazy-day things on the lawn behind our cottage, all except Grandma. She was sweeping spider webs off the outside of the cottage — the outside!

My father was putting golf balls into an overturned beer mug. "The Yanks can hit the moon in one blast," he muttered, "and I can't get a hole in one when all I've got to do is aim this damn ball straight for six feet."

The golf balls were rolling right by Schultz's nose, but he didn't even open his eyes. He just lay there like a limp sausage.

"We've got to go to see *Love Story* and *The Andromeda Strain* as soon as we get back to Regina," Mother said. "I sure hope they're still on." She was lying on a lounge reading the newspaper.

I was pretending a block of wood was a queen-sized bed with a canopy, the flowered paper serviette was a quilt, and a paper doll I'd cut out of last summer's Sears catalogue was a sleepy little witch called Tabitha, who was just going to bed. As I was covering Tabitha up, a dust devil danced by and blew both her and her quilt off the block of wood. I reached out to grab them, and Schultz leapt at me, snarling, teeth bared, and drooling.

He bit me on the chest. I screamed and shook him off. I couldn't believe he'd done it. But he jumped at me again, clamped his teeth through my T-shirt into my skin, and I was hitting and slapping him, screaming louder, and he was snarling and shaking his head back and forth. I could feel my skin being torn apart and I was really scared he'd kill me.

Then my parents were there, hitting him too, yelling at him to stop. And Schultz let go of me and flopped back down on the lawn.

Mother grabbed me up in her arms, then put me down again when I screamed she was hurting me. She looked at the bleeding mess on the front of my T-shirt and started to cry.

My father ran for the car keys, calling over his shoulder, "Get her into the car. Get her into the car. We'll take her down to Dr. Armstrong's."

Grandma ran up to the car with wet towels, wailing, "Oiy-oiy-oiy."

There was an awful lot of yelling. I was still screaming.

Jane came running up from the shore and she started screaming too when she saw the blood. Then she put her hand over her mouth, went over and sat down beside Schultz, and began stroking his back gently, asking him why he did it, telling him that he would have to say he was sorry.

My father carried me from the car down to Dr. Armstrong's cottage.

Dr. Armstrong looks like a bull dog and I shut my eyes when he lifted my shirt to look at the bites. He wanted to know what my father thought about the bloody NDP getting in again and taking off the utilization fees for hospital stays and visits to the doctor. When my father didn't answer, Dr. Armstrong said, "She's going to need stitches. Better take her up to Balcarres. They'll look after her. They've got a doctor on emergency at the hospital there."

"What about the dog?" my father asked. "Any danger he could be rabid?"

"Family pet?" Dr. Armstrong asked.

"Yes, yes," my father answered. "A dachshund we've had for ten years. A house dog, although he mouses under the cottage when we're out here."

"Oh, I wouldn't worry too much about that," Dr. Armstrong said. "She was probably teasing him. Watch the dog for the next week or two to be sure. But unless he shows fear of water, refuses to eat, foams at the mouth or takes a fit, I'd say you've got nothing to fear in that department."

By the time we got to Balcarres, the shock of Schultz attacking me had worn off a little bit, even if the pain from his bites hadn't. I was able to walk into the hospital between my mother and father.

I liked Dr. Peters right away. She looked like a Barbie doll — except her hair was cut short and it was brown, not blonde. The first thing she said was what a brave girl I was to walk into the hospital on my own two feet when I had wounds like that. She said any dog that bit someone that badly ought to be confined in a pen and watched carefully for any signs of rabies. She didn't accuse me of teasing Schultz and asking to be bitten.

VITAL STATISTIC

"Are you still okay, dear?" she kept asking. "I know this is strong antiseptic and it must hurt a lot, but I've got to get this wound cleaned up. You're certainly very brave."

I was trying not to breathe so it wouldn't hurt any more than it had to.

"Okay," she said. "That's over. Now, will you help me count the stitches?"

We counted seventeen.

Then she had to give me a needle in my seat. "You're braver than most men I've treated," she said, giving me a hug without squeezing me, just circling me with her arms. "Some of them act like real babies if I just ask them to stick out their tongue so I can see how much fur they've got on it." Of course, with her telling me how brave I was all the time, I didn't whimper once. I enjoyed being told I was brave. It made me feel grown up.

Schultz and I were kept apart from that Wednesday until Saturday. He was with Jane most of the time. On Saturday morning a family conference was called. Schultz wasn't in his usual place under the table and Grandma rubbed one slipper on the other.

My father said, "Schultz hasn't shown any signs of rabies whatsoever. He seems genuinely sorry. But we can't take a chance on him ever attacking anyone else like that. I think we have to take him to the vet in Balcarres and put him to sleep."

Well, Jane started it. Then everybody was crying — including me. Grandma crossed herself and said, "Oiy-oiy." My mother just let the sobs go, but Dad didn't cry out loud and that was worse. The water just ran out of his eyes and made spots like raindrops on his T-shirt. He was sitting very straight with his chest thrust out.

Dad and Jane took Schultz to the vet. The tears started rolling again when they told us about it. Schultz knew, they said. He licked Jane's hand all the way to the clinic. "He knew he was going to die, but he jumped right up on the vet's examination table," Jane said. "He was really brave. I hugged him while the needle went in. It just took a se. . .second and he was. . ." Then she got sort of hysterical and ran for her fort.

"She's very upset," Dad said. "And no wonder. I had to arrange for his head to be sent to Lethbridge for the rabies test. I had to. I had to be sure."

We were back in Regina when the long distance phone call came from Lethbridge the next Wednesday morning. Schultz was rabid. I was to be taken to a doctor immediately for rabies shots. Since a week had passed after the bite, I was in grave danger.

Dr. Hall, our family doctor in Regina, explained to me about the shots. He said he wasn't going to pull any punches because he knew

I was a brave girl. "Once the rabies virus gets into the body, the infection attacks the nerve tissues and will travel through them until it reaches the brain and death results," he said. "The only known way to prevent this is to inject ever-increasing amounts of vaccine so you'll build up an immunity that will destroy the virus before it reaches the brain. We're going to have to give you a series of shots in your stomach. Eight of them. One a day for eight days. You had a bad bite, close to your heart and to your brain. Okay? Do you understand the what and the why of the treatment?"

I said, "Yes. Eight is how old I am. I just had my birthday."

"Well, fine. You're almost grown up. This is going to hurt, but it will be over in a minute. We'll do a countdown together, shall we? We'll both keep a record so I don't make any mistakes and give you one shot too many," he said.

It was a huge needle, almost as big as the baster my mother used on the Sunday chicken. Dr. Hall winced when he stuck it into my stomach and pushed the plunger. Then he congratulated me for not screaming or crying. "You are a very courageous young lady," he said.

"Schultz was too," I said. "He knew that needle was going to kill him, my sister said so, but he jumped right up on the table and let the vet give it to him. My sister held him and hugged him until he died. But Schultz and I didn't get along very well. I wanted to tease him sometimes, but, honest, I never did. Everybody in our family really loved him a lot. If I get his rabies, will I die too?"

"The shots are going to prevent any chance of that — that's why we're putting you through this," Dr. Hall said.

Dr. Hall and I counted down to just one more shot — the Great Number Eight, we called it. Then another doctor called my parents. Mother said Dr. Davis knew more than anyone else about rabies because he'd lived in Africa for seventeen years. "He says the duck vaccine she's on isn't strong enough," she told my father.

"Why?" my father asked. "Because she's not quacking?"

He was trying to be funny, the same way I tried to be when Jane brought her friends over to see the black and blue marks the needles had left on my stomach. When they screamed and acted childish, I thrust my head toward them, snapped my teeth together, and said, "Look out, or I'll bite you and you'll have to get rabies shots too."

My mother didn't even smile at my father's remark. "Dr. Davis says we should consider switching her to the Semple vaccine. The stitches have put her at even more risk — the rabies virus might have been sewn into her. And . . . and, he says she could come down with rabies up to a *year* after being bitten so badly."

"Well we'd better take his advice and switch her to the Semple vaccine then," my father said. "Whatever that is."

"It'll still take a year to be sure she's out of danger," Mother said. "And there's something else. The Semple vaccine is a live virus grown in the embryo of a rabbit, but it could *cause* rabies too."

My mother started to cry. "What'll we do?" she said. "She'll have to start all over on a new series of eight shots and there's no guarantee. . ."

My parents thought I was in the kitchen with Grandma watching "Bewitched" on TV. They both jumped when I said, "I'll start the shots over if I have to. It's okay."

Dr. Hall told my father he couldn't make the decision. There are considerable risks either way, he said, but Dad finally got him to admit that if I were his little girl, he would follow Dr. Davis's advice.

On weekends, when the Medical Arts Clinic was closed, we went to the General Hospital Emergency for my shots. It was a different nurse each time. I think most of them wanted to practise giving rabies vaccine, until they saw the size of the needle and my black and blue stomach. Then they would turn white and shaky, holding back instead of getting it over with.

"Don't be afraid, just put 'er in — here!" I waved my finger around in diminishing circles, buzzing like a bee, and landed it on a spot between the worst bruises. One poor nurse had to close her eyes when she pushed the plunger.

Most of the time, being in grave danger wasn't much fun. All I was allowed to do was mope around the house and take it easy, get lots of rest, and stay quiet. I did get to go and see *Pinocchio* and *The Aristocats*, but I couldn't go to the Pile-o'-Bones Homecoming Sunday celebrations in the park. August was hot and we couldn't even go out to the cottage on weekends. I couldn't go with Jane to the pool either.

One day I caused a little excitement. I was sitting on the patio watching Jane dry her long hair. Grandma was in the vegetable garden, bent over like a coolie, picking weeds. Jane was in her bathing suit and Grandma was wearing her backless sun dress. Suddenly I was itchy everywhere. The mosquitoes were eating me alive, I said. I went inside and complained about them to Mother. She called out the window to Grandma and Jane and asked if the mosquitoes were bothering them. Jane said she hadn't seen a mosquito all day. Grandma said neither had she. But I was covered with lumps from head to toe. Mother ran to the phone and called Dr. Hall's office.

The next thing I knew, I was in the bathtub with a bag of oatmeal and a whole box of baking soda that Mother had poured into the water.

Everyone was standing there watching me as if I was going to die of rabies right in front of their eyes.

Dr. Hall came and examined me. He said that I'd had a reaction to one of the drugs mixed in with the Semple vaccine, that it wasn't the first signs of rabies at all, or anything that was life-threatening, just uncomfortable hives. He had to go over his diagnosis several times, even though the whole family was in the bathroom to hear him the first time.

I only cried once during the whole time I was getting the shots. That was when I overheard my mother ask my father to do her a favour. "Please. Take this old medical text I inherited from Dad and hide it from me for a year. Will you? Please?"

"Why?" Dad asked.

"It's so awful. Louis Pasteur's efforts to find a cure for hydrophobia. Some handwritten notes about a little black boy in Alabama that got rabies after being bitten by a dog. They had to lock him up in a warehouse until he died because he was too wild to go near. It's so horrible." My mother started to cry and I'm never brave when that happens. I always start to cry too. It scares me. And I didn't want to die like the little black boy.

"Lord Almighty," Dad said. "That was a million years ago, before duck and rabbit vaccines. Don't worry. She's okay."

"She'll be nine years old before we're sure. Nine!" My mother thrust the book at him and went upstairs to their bedroom.

So you see, my ninth birthday was crucial. I made it through my eighth year without getting rabies from Schultz or from the Semple vaccine.

The best birthday card I got came from Dr. Hall and Dr. Davis. It has a cardinal on the front of it, a bright red one in full flight with a banner shaped like a nine in its beak. The Saskatchewan rabies statistics for 1971 are stapled inside. It says on them that they were compiled for the provincial epidemiologist, Dr. E.C. Davis. But I think they were compiled for me — and for Schultz too, in a way.

In the first column it shows that one eight-year-old female was bitten by a rabid dog, "domestic pet", it says in brackets. It doesn't say that the dog could jump really high, that he was completely housebroken, could roll over, shake a paw, or that he'd never bitten anyone except me. Schultz is just a statistic. His name isn't even there, but then neither is mine. In brackets after "female" it says "survived" — and that's underlined in red ink with two exclamation points behind it.

In handwriting on the card, though, it says, "Happy Birthday to a courageous young lady — a very *vital* statistic."

Playboy

Put 'er there, pal. I'm a Top Ten Man. That's what the TTM stands for on this business card, next door to my name. Been on the team five years — right since I made the shirt and tie brigade. You understand what that means?

Could be only another runt sired by a slippery Scot out of a thoroughbred Ukrainian would get the real glory of that. Mac, my old man, dropped by the Symetzki homestead seven times before he hopped the rails for good. Ma says I just squirted out onto her brother's sheepskin coat seven months and seven days after the CPR took Mac away. I'm lucky number seven of the MacSymetzki boys he left with her to raise. Always figured that's as good as being the seventh son of the seventh son, luck-wise.

Muscled my way from Dysart to the Queen City at age fifteen. Worked for an outfit called Donald Duck Delivery when I first hit Regina. Knew how to put my best foot forward even as a kid. Pedalled an old CCM delivering meat to the south end's prime cuts for five cents a trip, winter and summer. Sent money home to Ma in Dysart, too.

The big break was getting on with Zephyr Industrial Products. ZIP's cleaning and sanitary products sweep the east and get you the best wipe in the west, like I say. Hustled myself up from errand boy, to stock, to repairs, to sales by age forty-seven. My TTM's earned. It matters. You know what I mean?

Anyways, the reason I look like this doesn't mean what you think. I netted my TTM all right, all right. Did it by scoring a hat trick in this year's quota game. ZIP laid on a mid-winter calypso in the sun as number one prize to hype the old sales incentive. Not that a guy like me needs hyping to move the merchandise, you understand. But when ZIP offers the Top Ten Men from across Canada a five-day jaunt to Jamaica for re-lax-ation, if you know what I mean, a guy like me leads the pack. Right? Right!

ZIP always whips up a first class trip for us TTMs. We each get one of these Happy Face buttons, gold with black letters: *HELLO! My name is Emil J. (Super Uke) MacSymetzki, Sales Rep. South Sask.* Pretty classy, eh? Friendly touches like using our nicknames shows how it's no expense spared for ZIP's TTMs. You can see that, eh?

Well, old Bronco Berenson from South Alberta and a new TTM from Fog Coast somewheres were on my flight out of home base in Regina. Bronco I know from way back, but Peter R. Mathews-Moore from B.C. looked right off to be an exception to the old ZIP-zip. First off, there's no nickname on his Happy Face button. That's suspicious, know what I mean? Then he's got a briefcase full of sales charts he hauls out with the company's bonus catalogue and he pokes his thin nose into them like they were *Stag* magazine. St. Pete even turns down the free booze and asks the stew for a Montclair cocktail, which Bronco tells me's just plain water jacked-up with minerals and a hunk of lemon. St. Pete comes across as aloof, you know what I mean? Stuck up, that's for sure.

Anyways, the boys from down east turn out to be real shoulder-to-shoulder men. No surprise in that, neither. ZIP's always been kind of a family as much as a business to us guys. You know what I mean? None of this wine and dine and hire the wife too, like IBM.

Our human resources department just wants to know their men got a little woman at home to look after the care and feeding and assorted private essentials. ZIP appreciates that. Wives of us Top Ten Men get to pick a waffle iron, toaster, fry pan, any item they fall in love with out of the "B" section of the Bonus Catalogue. There's nothing they'd want in the "A" section, that's for sure. It's golf clubs, suitcases, car and office stuff for us men. The "B" section's set up to keep the little woman happy fixing her kitchen while her TTM re-laxes.

I want to tell you that four-hour flight Toronto-Jamaica was lively as our ZIP Friday night get-togethers at the Empire pub back home. I led the sing-song, "Down by the seaside siftin sand. . ." I pumped a little Al Jolson in with my Belafonte to ac-cen-tuate the matched set of Happy Face smiles I'm displaying, "I'd walk a million miles for one of your —"

"Hey, Super Uke," Tidy Ted Thompson from Bay Street in Metro T.O. calls out. "The seat belt sign's on. Douse the cigar and sit down, pal."

"One more time," I tell Tidy, getting up from my Jolson-kneel for the finale. "Mary Anne, Mary Anne. . . and here goes!"

Old Bronco holds out his arm in the aisle again for the Super Uke Limbo Special. I hump right under it and on down past six or seven more seats beneath the other arms that shoot out.

I gotta thank my daily 5BX, and the fact my centre of gravity's low, for making me flex-i-ble. I'm just not built to stiff and solemn like St. Pete, a guy who's at least a dozen years younger than me. I figure it pays off to keep the old Super Uke muscles moving and a smile on my face to match right up with my Happy Face button. I practised the limbo under the wife's ZIP broom a couple of weekends but never got near as low as on that airplane. Back of my head damn near touched the carpet and I did a U-turn to limbo back to my seat, no problem at all.

"Mr. MacSymetzki! Sir? Please take your seat and fasten your belt. We're on final approach." The stacked stew with the sour-o mouth grabbed hold of the collar of my new orange-striped shirt and tried to pull me up on my feet.

I give her my ZIP sales-pitch smile, all nine hundred and eighty-five bucks worth of Doc McIvor's shiny porcelain caps for the big dazzle, plus the pinch she's been asking for on her tight little ass.

"Re-lax, babe," I tell her as she keeps grappling me. "Enjoy! Guess we know what she needs, eh Bronco?" I say.

"Fly me," Bronco says to her. "Cowboys stay up longer."

The stew's mouth opens into a capital O. She grabs Bronco's glass and snarls something about ZIP men being worse than the apes on a football club charter. Then we're on the ground.

Since I'm still standing, I'm just nat-ur-ally the first TTM to bongo-bongo down that ramp into the Kingston sun.

Turns out the ZIP hotel's the Half Moon, clear across the island in Ocho Rios. St. Pete lines up two cabs before we've knocked back seconds of that rum punch Jamaica welcome. We chug-a-lug and pile in. I'm first in our car, up front with the driver. I gotta admit that was a hair-y ride. I'm used to doing my own steering, you know what I mean? And it's on Sask roads straight as a ZIP mop handle. Anyways, I keep smiling with this tidal wave of over-proof rum sloshing right to left in my gut as we careen round those mountains. Sounds like the ocean's inside of me. Feels like it too, know what I mean?

St. Pete's sitting smack behind me, calling, "Tilt!" like he's enjoying it when our side of the cab leans out over what's gotta be the world's rockiest drop into ob-liv-ion. I mean, two squealing doughnuts of rubber are the only things holding us onto terra firma. First off, I figure his mineral cocktails have silted his peewee brain. I take a look back next time he yells and see he's about ready to up-chuck over my shoulder. St. Pete's right up on the edge of the seat and his face is white as a roll of ZIP toilet paper.

"You gotta garp, stick your head out the window," I yell at him. "I got on my new hundred per cent virgin polyester tropical suit." I reach back and roll down his window. "You should of been drinking the joy-juice and moving round on the flight down, not reading," I say. "Hang your head out there. The ZIP travel list said bring one suit and that's all I've got. On me. Don't want it mucked up with barf."

All the time I'm trying to talk him into aiming his mouth over the cliffs, I'm thinking St. Pete's likely got those two pet bags he pulls behind him on a leash full of tropical silk suits. You know what I mean? But he's rolling his window up as we lay into a curve that almost throws me onto the driver's lap. Everyone except St. Pete and me yells, "Tilt!", the driver included. I try a little ZIP buddy-to-buddy gab on him to get him to slow down. "You a cum lawda grad of the Indianapolis 500?" I ask.

He shows a keyboard of teeth pearlier than my caps and I swear he steps on the gas. I shut up. Every time the ZIP men in the cab behind us get close enough they could give us a back-slap, our man burns the rubber and gives us another tilt.

By the time we get to the Half Moon, we're greener than ZIP liquid deodorizer. You could've lost any one of us in that jungle of house plants around the entrance and no trace.

Anyways, we get re-laxed right off. I get a bar set up in my room before some of the guys behind us turn the keys in their doors. St. Pete sips soda like the wife does and keeps putting in his two bits worth about some sort of new ZIP image the company's going to cultivate. Takes me about half-way through dinner to get the jokes rolling. But I showed St. Pete how to cult-i-vate, know what I mean?

We wound up the first night playing poker on my patio till dawn, the splash of the booze going into our glasses louder than the sea lapping away at the sand. St. Pete took the pot, which was enough to send me off to the sack stone cold sober, if you know what I mean.

ZIP had the works laid on for golf at 9 a.m. — clubs, caddies, carts, free booze flowing at the ninth and nineteenth holes. I figured they would, so I set a fast pace. "You gotta move the old stick, men. Make it a TTM's game. This ain't the bush league. Elbows up and make like it's a little white puck you're shooting," I yelled at the slow swingers. "Dysart Dynamites're still looking for a guy fast as old Super Uke here in the face-off."

I don't mind admitting my score was lousy, but I kept the boys en-ter-tained. St. Pete tried to damp things down with looks thick as

B.C. fog. Not a smile shone through till he collected the winner's bucks at the last hole. And that was more smirk than smile.

I took a TTM poll back at the hotel. "Siesta or swim? Wanta zonk out or jump in with the bathing beauties?"

"In!" old Bronco yelled, holding his nose. "It'll give us some practice for the Playboy bunnies tonight."

St. Pete was at the pool when we got there. He kept running up the ladder to the high diving board, flexing his puny muscles, and doing fancy dives off it like he was in some sort of ballet or something. He danced around on his toes, arms fluttering above his head, doing imitations of a swan when he dived. He was wearing some sort of a G-string instead of real manly swim shorts. Tidy Ted said it was a jockstrap and I said I'd never seen one that small. They'd of arrested me for wearing it, know what I mean?

The wife picked me up a pair of real he-man boxer-style trunks with a matching terry-lined shirt. Sure, I could've done without sunflower blooms splashed all over me, but they hid the bulge of the family jewels from envious eyes, which was probably what the little woman had in mind.

Anyways, I doffed the shirt and dunked into the shallow end right away. I swam round with my feet hardly touching the bottom at all. The way I do it, thrashing round like a whale, flopping up and down, and hanging the odd sunflower moon or two with my hands on the bottom, no one could tell I don't swim a stroke. Soon as my skin got wrinkled, I rose from the shallows and grabbed me a middle-front lounge close to some real dolls. TNT and a TTM!

The other guys were there before I could strike up a conversation. So we lay round the pool spreading some re-part-ee on the upcoming night at the Playboy Club. The boys pumped me for the facts about Bunny School training. Like I told them, I buy *Playboy* for the cartoons. But one month the first article jumps right off the page at me like a bare bum. Turns out to be all about Bunny lessons. Like I said to the boys, those chicks take lessons on how to do this bump and grind routine so they can waggle their bums in your face after they bring your drinks. I stood up and shook my field of sunflowers at the boys to demonstrate. A flicker of de-lights to come hopped through a few TTM minds from what I could see, if you know what I mean. Gave us something to con-cen-trate on when St. Pete quit diving and started boring us with some lesson he'd learned in a *Financial Post* article. I mean, in Jamaica? Can you believe a stunned wimp like him works for ZIP? No way, eh?

Anyways, I went up in plenty of time to shower, shave, and spray up a storm in honour of Bunny bums to come. Must of splashed on half a bottle of Brut. That stuff hurts like hell on a sunburn, too. I want to tell you my skin was red as what's left of my hair. Even my new tropical suit felt like barbed wire.

I hammered doors down until I got all the TTMs rounded up. I led them down to the Half Moon bar to wait for the wagon to Bunnyland. I showed the waiter how to deliver our drinks Bunny-style. He was *one of those*, if you know what I mean, and did it real good. Gave us a good laugh, anyways. We were wound pretty tight when the Express to Bunny Heaven got there.

"Wouldn't you know it?" I say to the boys. "This time we get a driver who'd lag behind in a funeral procession."

"Go, man, go," Bronco yells, and the boys join in, stamping their feet and snorting like bulls.

Then St. Pete's gotta butt into the fun. "We're early," he says, looking at his watch. "Our reservation is for nine o'clock." Next thing you know he's boring us stiff with Jamaican history, pointing out old buildings like this was some sort of ed-u-cation-al lecture tour. Dates, names, everything. Boring facts. Bor-ing.

Anyways, I led the way into the Playboy Club.

Took a few secs to focus the old eyeballs, you know what I mean?

Plush? Made the Hotel Sask look like Len's Greasy Spoon in Ogema, no kidding.

"We're gonna need a seeing-eye dog to lead us through this shag carpet," Bronco says.

"No dogs in this hutch," I tell him. My old ticker's going like a 400-cube V8 at fast idle.

Then this fluffy cottontail, all dimples and curves, nuzzles on up to us and whispers, "The gentlemen from Zephyr Industrial Products? I'm Bunny Penny. I'm your Bunny for the evening. Will you please follow me to your reserved table?"

Would we! My V8 surged into overdrive, you know what I mean? I glommed the old headlights onto Bunny Penny and tailgated her right to the table.

Like I told the boys earlier, I'm a bum man. Floppy, waffled, dimpled, or smooth, a waggling bum gets me where I live. I've got a bumper-wide Happy Face grin of Doc McIvor's gold, chrome and pure porcelain caps that would've blown a gasket on a Rolls Royce.

"Hey, Bronco," I say, without turning around. "Bugs Bunny she's not!"

"And th-that's not all f-f-folks," Bronco stutters like a Looney Tune cartoon character. "I wah-wah-wasted six years working for an outfit that suh-suh-sent whole families to Duh-Duh-Disneyland as a suh-suh-sales in-cen-tive. Loo-loo-loony, eh?"

From what I see, Hugh Hefner's got a TTM blueprint of real in-cen-tive.

We gotta go down three steps to a kidney-shaped couch that's covered with fur. Shaggy fur. Blonde. And there's this long table, curved to fit it, covered with fur too. Short fur. Curly. Blonde like on the couch. I run my fingers through it, guiding myself to front row centre. And I sit, ging-er-ly. It's like being in a fur-lined womb and looking out at Bunny Penny, crotch-level. You know what I mean? Hefner'd get arrested in Canada for thinking about it, wouldn't he? Eh?

ZIP TTMs crowd in on either side of me. I want to tell you I'm grinning ear to ear, stroking the short ones on the table, waiting for when she turns and waggles her plump little cheeks at me. I don't plan to grab. No way. Just a gentleman's pat where it counts, is what's going round in my mind.

"Something special from the bar, gentlemen?" Bunny Penny asks it like she's French-kissing each word.

"Spesh-ul!" I growl, adjusting the family jewels.

"Yeah, special-special," the other TTMs chorus.

Bunny Penny turns and bounces her cute little button tail off into the dark.

"She forgot her bump and grind," I say.

"And to take my order for a Virgin Mary," St. Pete says.

Can you believe it? In the Playboy Club this guy's looking for a virgin anything? He's coiled into his spot at the end of the table and glares at me as if it's my fault virgins and milk aren't the feature attractions.

"Hey! Lookit this! Bunny Penny got our orders," Bronco says.

Bunny Penny appears in front of us again in the pink spotlight. She's carrying a tray full of giant glasses that're piled up with more fruit than Carmen Miranda's turban.

"Ten Playboy Specials, gentlemen." She's got a voice like a dove's coo, no kidding. She's over by St. Pete but looking down at me, smiling, recognizing that dead centre on that couch is a leader of TTMs. I'm flashing the porcelain and thinking about the tan-tal-izing bummy-flick I'm going to get when I hear St. Pete mutter, "Tilt!"

Bunny Penny stumbles. The tray's edge gets bigger and bigger, spinning toward me like a giant puck. Before I can shut my gaping grin to protect my TTM bridgework, it hits.

Nine hundred and eighty-five bucks worth of ZIP Happy Face smile cracks its moorings and explodes in a spray of shrapnel. The Playboy Specials hit me in the face, pour into my ears, onto my shoulders, chin, chest, paunch. Enough rum to float the fleet hits my lap. Ice cold! Hunks of orange, grapefruit, pineapple, lemon, lime and shaved ice crash down on me like the Niagara Falls. Worse, the glasses hit the edge of the table and shatter themselves into spikes of deadly shards that shoot down the rum rapids to spear a man's pride, the wife's joy, you know what I mean? Then I feel parts of Doc's built-for-ZIP smile biting their way down my gullet.

ZIP TTMs peel off the couch on both sides of me. I stand up slow-ly, care-ful-ly, letting the glass, fruit, ice and rum run off of me.

Pink satin bunnies pop out of holes in the darkness.

The manager appears in the spotlight, wringing a wine cloth. "Sir? Our apologies, sir. I'll personally drive you to your hotel to change. Your drinks are on the house."

I tip rum out of my new white patent shoes, touch my fingers to my mouth.

What's left of my ZIP sales smile are these fangs, the ones Doc filed into points to hold the caps. I wanta give the old A-okay smile to Bunny Penny, you know what I mean? She's standing there bawling like a calf. But that's going to frighten her worse. I know that. She sees a Super Uke Vampire grinning at her and she's going to faint dead away. I got no trouble hearing her through the banana slices and pineapple chunks in my ears. She's sobbing, "Your-your feet. I didn't see your feet, sir," as St. Pete leads her away saying he'll speak to Mr. Hefner himself so she won't get fired.

Me and the rest of the ZIP TTMs are left to act like the last of the great white hunters. We scare up a few bits of my smile out of the shaggy fur of the carpet. It's nowhere near enough to fix up my Super Uke Happy Face grin.

Anyways, turns out Jamaican dentists are scarce as palm trees in the Queen City. Plus, I've got a serious concern about just how the dental works I swallowed are going to reappear. You know what I mean? Going down was bad enough. Coming out was going to be something else, what with my piles and all. Sure, the hotel doctor looked me over. But he did it so fast I figure he must of been a brother of the driver that got us to the Half Moon. Kept on grinning and shaking his head like he thought I was doomed to be ripped to shreds by my own teeth, then took off.

ZIP Human Resources came to the rescue. They got me this special death-case priority to grab this flight home. Guess I gotta admit St. Pete made a few long distance calls about it.

Anyways, it's my new polyester tropical suit I got on that smells bad. Not me. Festered fruit and dried rum smells rotten, all right. Sort of dead smelling, eh? All those virgin polyesters being defiled like that don't help, ha, ha. Thing is, takes weeks to get anything dry-cleaned down there in Jamaica.

But, you know something? I'm feeling as bad as I smell and look. The stews on this flight might as well be bumless for all I care. I'm somber and sober as St. Pete. It's him that comes to mind every time I catch a broad's backside in the old headlamps now. It's on account of what he did and what I figure he's going to try next.

Lookit this. You see what it says right here in the *Globe's* B.S.? Front page of it, no less?

"Peter Roger Mathews-Moore named National Sales Manager of Zephyr Industrial Products."

Goes on to tell how he's set to clean up ZIP's marketing system and sanitize its sales force to attract college grads. And that's not all, neither. Turns out his little woman's a favourite niece of ZIP's Pres and *she* wants to get involved in the business.

I'm telling you, this article gives me a sniff of a whole new ass-pect of ZIP's old happy family.

Anyways, there's one thing for sure. And you'd better believe it. I'm not called Super Uke or got this TTM next door to my name for nothing. You know what I mean?

In The Middle

My name is Nell Harris-Nelson. I'm almost eleven, in Grade 6, and I'm seriously thinking about dropping out of school to be a writer. My parents say I've got a lot of talent. They just found that out when I gave Mom her Mother's Day card early. Before that, except for report card time, they really didn't pay much attention to what I was doing.

You see, I'm their middle daughter — the one who gets squeezed out of sight by a thirteen-year-old Brooke Shields look-alike and an eight-year-old with Orphan Annie eyes.

If I was an only child, I guess they would have found out a long time ago that I was good at something besides drawing. I'll bet an only child could bring home a bag of alley cats and her parents would jump right up to give her the money to buy kitty litter. Oldest and youngest kids have things like that happen too. Middle kids don't.

Middle is invisible — especially if you're stuck between Queen Blue Jeans and Little Princess Big Eyes. Most of the time, it's like being the hole in a doughnut.

But I got used to it. I knew exactly where I stood. There was no doubt about it, I figured, my mom loved my older sister and my younger sister an awful lot better than me. It was pretty obvious. When she didn't have to read a stack of books for the English class she takes, write another essay, cook, clean, wash our clothes and stuff, her so-called Quality Time was spent on them. I noticed. It didn't bother me much, though. Just a fact of life in the centre slot, I thought, and I concentrated on the comic strip I'm drawing about a girl nobody in her family notices until she grows up to be the first woman prime minister of Canada.

And my dad? Well, he's at home a lot marking papers and stuff because he teaches political science at the university. He loves the dog best and the rest of us about equally, I'd say. That's fair enough, I guess. Che Guevara is the only other male in our family and he's about the same age as my dad. Actually, Che is six human-years old, times seven, so he's a few years younger than my dad. And you won't catch Che going around flexing his knee joints, moaning about how tough it is to keep the poor old bod in shape, or whimpering about a few hairs falling out. Che is a very handsome German shepherd and acts as if he knows it. My dad's not bad looking either, considering his age and his receding hairline.

My mom is a lot younger than Dad or Che. She likes to make that clear to us. She says her knee joints are just fine *because* she hates boring exercise programs. She refuses, positively and definitely, to go jogging with a couple of old dogs no matter how handsome they are. I've heard her say that often enough to know she means it. Lying on the chesterfield stroking a cat and turning the pages of a good novel are her favourite exercises, she says.

Our first cat just happened to follow my little sister home from school. Mom was suspicious about that right away.

"How could this beautiful big cat follow you when you're carrying it?" she asked, taking it from Amy's clutches to cuddle it. The cat scrambled up her sweater and tried to hide in her long hair.

"I walked backwards all the way," Amy said, opening her eyes wider than Orphan Annie's.

You know, I have to hand it to that kid. My eyes get all squinty when I try to make up excuses. Amy's not dumb. She doesn't tell fibs. And she almost never has to whine or throw a tantrum to get what she wants. She just turns those big blue spotlights on Mom or Dad and waits for them to melt. They always do. It happened again. Mom put an ad in the newspaper describing the cat Amy found. But, when nobody called, she said I didn't have to bother drawing posters for IGA and Safeway. Amy got to keep her cat and Mom named it Suspicious.

My dad and Che weren't very fond of Suspicious. To tell you the truth, they don't like cats much. Che tried to get playful with Suspicious a few times, bouncing around her with that silly grin and fake snarl. It made her hiss for so long Amy thought her cat was going to go flat. Once in a while, Dad complained about Mom letting Suspicious sneak up on their bed and sleep on her pillow, nestled in her hair. That damn cat's so close to our faces, Dad said, it could steal our breath away and suffocate us or give us fur balls in our stomachs. Mostly, though, Dad and Che were able to ignore the fact that a cat had joined our family — until the Sunday morning Amy turned poor Suspicious into a wildcat.

Afterwards, Amy told me she was pretending the living room was a Pretty Pets Beauty Sal*oon* and hadn't meant to scare Suspicious out of her wits. I believe her. Like I said, she doesn't tell fibs. What Amy did was pump mousse all over Suspicious and, when it dried so fast the cat felt ceramic, she used every last dab of my older sister's brand-new giant economy size jar of zit cream trying to make the mousse vanish. The poor cat went wild and the noise woke the rest of us up. We could hear the sound of things breaking, Che barked as if burglars had broken into the house, and Amy was shouting and swearing like a university student.

By the time we got down to the living room, my Mom's Cicansky cabbage and a table lamp were smashed; Suspicious had smeared zit cream on everything and was trying to climb the Venetian blinds; and Che was so confused he was chasing his tail and howling whenever he caught it. My older sister, Jessica — (pardon me, she'd changed her name to Jessi that weekend) — my sister Jessi freaked right out. Queen Jessi stood in the middle of the room screaming. Without mousse to set her hair, she said she couldn't poke her nose out of the house. And she screamed that acne was breaking out all over her face, she could feel the pimples popping. I was really tempted to ask her how much mousse she needed to set the hairs in her nose, but she was already hysterical.

When we finally caught Suspicious and got her into the bathtub, we had to use Tide, Mr. Clean, shampoo, and some of my dad's special hair restorative cream rinse to get the gunk off her fur. After we dried her with Mom's hair blower, Suspicious looked like the same fluffy grey Persian cat as before, but she didn't act the same. She tried to hide from us by slithering under things that would have scraped the skin off a snake's back.

I spent a lot of time looking for Suspicious and coaxing her to come out of her hiding places. It's not that I'm some kind of saint or anything. I don't mean you should believe that. In a way, it was something better to do than my homework, that's all. You see, I'm the poor student in our family. Sister Anne says I clown around too much in class. She even did a novena for me. She went to mass every first Friday for nine months to ask God to smarten me up. He didn't though. I'm still getting Fs for "Attitude". But what makes me mad at God is, He let me fail Suspicious too, right when she needed me most.

It was just before Jessy — (yes, I'm almost sure she was Jessy by then) — started Grade 9 at LeBoldus High School. We were going to the Golden Mile Mall to buy her a new outfit for the first day. Her closet was full of new things, but nothing she thought was just right. I was sort of interested in what Jessy bought because I usually have to wear stuff she doesn't like while it's practically still warm. I'll tell you one thing, I'm going to Marian High School if I ever graduate from St. John's because it's all girls and they wear uniforms. Shopping bores me as much as exercise programs bore my mom. I wanted to get it over with and I didn't take time to do my usual check to see where Suspicious hid after I let her out. I just shoved Amy into the back seat of the car and climbed in behind her.

"What was that?" Mom asked, as she was backing out of the carport. "*Somebody* left runners on the trunk again!"

She meant me. I was the only one who'd ever done that. But, before I could get mad at being blamed unfairly, we saw Suspicious on the driveway in front of us. She was sort of thrashing around and all bloody.

Mom slammed on the brakes, kind of fell out against her door as she opened it, and cried, "Oh, my God, my God! I've run over her! Oh, my God! My God! What'll I do?" She was taking wobbly steps forwards and backwards, hanging onto the door.

Mr. Wilson, the retired farmer next door, was digging the potatoes he plants in his front yard instead of grass. He came running, using his spade like a crutch because of his game leg.

"Holy Jesus!" he said. "I thought it was one of the girls! Take the children and go inside. I'll finish her off and bury her. Them damn barn cats get up under the fenders," he said. He took my mom's arm and steered her around the back of the car to the front door of the house so she wouldn't have to walk past Suspicious. We followed, crying.

Mom rushed straight to the phone and called my dad at the university. She said it was an emergency at home. By the time my dad got from the lecture theatre to the department office telephone, she was practically hysterical. "Ernie? Oh, God, Ernie, there's been a horrible accident here," she sobbed. "I ran over her on the driveway and oh God it was such a little bump that I thought it was just runners again and . . . " She was crying too hard to talk.

I took the phone from her. "Daddy? It was Suspicious and Mr. Wilson says she was . . ." But he'd hung up. The dial tone purred in my ear.

My dad ran into the kitchen five minutes later, stumbling over Che and not even stopping to apologize. Amy was on Mom's lap and he wrapped his arms around them, kissing them both, even though their noses were running. "It's okay, it's okay," he kept saying. "Thank God you're all safe." He reached out and hugged Jessy and me into the huddle. "Wilson looked after it. He's even hosing down the driveway. Thank God it was just that damn cat! It shouldn't have been under your car in the first place."

I know my dad didn't mean to make me feel worse, but he did. What if I'd remembered to look for Suspicious? What if I'd thought to feel under the fenders? What if I'd just left my runners on the trunk again? Mom wouldn't have killed me. What if? What if? The accident wouldn't have happened! That's all I could think of when I went to bed.

Mom and I both had nightmares about it. Mine were in slow motion without any sounds: the soft bump, Suspicious squirming, blood oozing, Mr. Wilson raising his spade up. I had to fight to open my eyes before he brought the spade down on her head. It was as if it was all happening deep at the bottom of a cold lake, under water, and I was drowning. I don't know what my mom's nightmares were like. We didn't talk about them. But she looked pretty awful some mornings and Dad kept telling her to forget about what had happened to that damn cat.

My older sister, what's-her-name, thought of a way to help Mom forget the tragic accident. She brought a kitten home and hid it in her closet to give Mom on her birthday as a surprise. Normally, Jess or Jessy or Jessi or Jessica — (I can never remember what she's calling herself so I'll just call her Jess) — *Jess* usually had a tantrum if Amy or I even dared to knock on the door of her private space, which is what she calls her bedroom. But she told us to go right in there any old time to keep the kitten from meowing. You know, except for her problem deciding on her name, my older sister is really smart as well as great looking. But Mom's birthday was a month away and that kitten had a meow that sounded like bagpipes tuning up. So Jess's surprise didn't work. The kitten got lonesome stuffed into her closet with all those shoes and clothes on the floor and meowed so loudly the very first night that Mom went in to investigate. And, of course, she took her new kitten to bed with her to snuggle.

My dad named the new family member Mao Tse-tung because of her mournful meow. She was a super-smart cat, part Burmese, which was why she had one orange eye and one blue one, Jess said. Mao was all black except for two white tufts over both ears just like my dad has. Dad said cats weren't loyal or trustworthy, like dogs, and that Mao was the rare exception that proved the rule. Mao was at the door with Che to greet Dad when he came home from lecturing, and she even went jogging with them.

"We make quite a trio," Dad told Mom, shaking his head and grinning. "That cat's just like a little dog. After the first time around our route she was leading us. And, you don't have to worry about her, Che looks after her when we're running as if she was his pup."

When Dad watches the TV supper time news, he demands complete and utter silence from all of us, but he let Mao curl up on his lap and purr like a jet engine. He just zapped up the volume on the set and didn't say a word. Sometimes Mao hung down from Dad's creaky knees and took swipes at Che's wagging tail, or licked Che's ears whenever he perked them up like a purebred's.

We're sure that what got Mao was the German shepherd across the street, the one that keeps breaking loose from his chain. How would Mao know a dog that looked so much like Che was vicious? Dad found Mao at the foot of the poplar tree where he goes to stretch his muscles before his morning jog. Actually, Dad and Che found Mao lying there. Che wouldn't leave her body or stop whimpering — it was a keen, not a whimper or a whine. Mom blamed herself for letting Mao out that morning and for having her declawed so she wouldn't scratch up the furniture like Suspicious did. It was as bad as losing a child, Mom and Dad kept saying, hugging each other. They were calm and deliberate about burying Mao and sad all the time afterwards.

Dad and Che didn't go jogging that weekend, or on Monday morning either. I didn't want to go to school, but the first thing I saw when I got into the classroom was the notice Sister Anne let Lisa put up on the blackboard: *KITTENS FOR SALE $1*, it said. I was sure it was a message from God for me. My school project for Mother's Day was almost finished, but I didn't like it much. We were supposed to do an illustrated essay on "Why I Love My Mother" for language arts. I'd written things about my mom being so young and having such long hair kittens could hide in it. That part was okay, I thought. My drawings were what was awful. I couldn't get her pretty enough. It was her lips or her teeth or something. My mom smiles a lot, but my drawings made her look as if she was snarling.

I chose the cute little calico kitten no one else at Lisa's was petting. Its meow was so soft I could have kept it hidden under my mom's nose for a week. But I was so excited I wanted to give it to her right away. Sister Anne said children didn't need to wait for commercial gift days to give their mothers a gift of love.

"Hey, Mom! Surprise! Got a present for you," I called when I got home. Che stood on his hind legs and sniffed, but he didn't growl or bark.

Oh, one thing I forgot to say. It was almost report card time and I'd made some promises to at least get a D or a C in Attitude.

So, at first, I thought my mom was just surprised I wasn't waving my report card over my head. I held the kitten out to her and Mom's face turned into one of my ugly drawings.

"Oh no you don't," she said, putting her hands behind her back. "I'll never touch another kitten as long as I live. You take it back, Nell. Back to wherever you got it!"

"I can't, Mom," I said. "I bought it for you for Mother's Day. This is my gift of love to make you feel happy again."

"Take it back!" my mom said.

"Here, Mom, feel how soft she is," I said, holding the kitten out to her. "And look at the colours. My kitten isn't just grey or black — she's a rainbow!"

"Nell! Take it right back to where you found it," Mom said, and turned her back on me.

Lisa could tell I'd been crying because my eyes were all red. I squinted them up and said my mom had just discovered I had an allergy to calico cats. I knew Lisa didn't believe me. She said okay, she would take the kitten back, and I could return the dollar's worth of kitty litter she'd let me fill my lunch pail with too, but she couldn't give me a refund. She said that she'd already spent my two dollars on perfume to give her mother for Mother's Day so I would just have to wait for the next batch of kittens and choose one that I wasn't allergic to. I didn't argue with her.

When I got home again, I marched right past my mom as if she was invisible and went upstairs into Jessica's bedroom. I took my older sister's black marking pen and printed *JESSICA* on the outside of her door in big letters. Then I helped myself to some of her green bristol board, used her manicure scissors to cut it into postcard sizes, found her stapler behind a stack of *Seventeen* magazines and fastened the cards together at the top, and sat down at her dressing table to write my Mother's Day card:

> Mom! You are the one
> I don't love.
> I could tell when
> you first saw my
> present that you
> loved that kitten.
> (over)

> Don't worry because
> I'll remember what a
> mean Mom you are.
> That's what I'll tell
> my children. Just
> think what my friends
> (over)

> will say when I tell
> them you wouldn't let me
> keep one harmless little
> kitten even when I paid
> for it. I paid $1 for
> (over)
>
> that cat. That's 2 dollars
> down the drain because $1
> was for kitty litter.
> Thanks a lot!
> I'm going to hate
> you forever, Mom!
> Love, Me

I waited until a long time after my parents were in bed before I shot the card under their door. I heard it hit the dresser leg like a brick. One of them got up and got it, because I heard the bed creak — and creak again, as whoever it was got back into bed again. It was my mom who read it aloud I think, really low, almost a whisper, and then it sounded as if they were both laughing.

I tiptoed back to my bedroom, turned on my light, and started to make plans to run away as soon as the sun was up. I was going to go somewhere I would be visible, and loved, and have a calico cat of my very own. I was just thinking I should take Che with me, and maybe Amy, when my parents burst into my room without even knocking and threw themselves down on my bed at either side of me.

"*Love, me,*" Mom said. "That's the most beautiful hate letter I've ever read. It's literature!"

"It is," Dad said. "She ought to get the Governor-General's Award."

"Oh, honey," Mom said, hugging me, "I'm sorry. I'm just not ready to think about having another cat yet. But I'll shrivel up and die if you hate me forever for that."

"Me too," Dad said, "and you know how old I am — shedding my hair all over the place. But the old mind's not gone yet. I'll get it in shape to welcome a new cat before long — you can count on it. And I'll speak to Che about what kind we'd like."

"Have I ever told you that you're my favourite middle daughter?" Mom asked. She gave me a hug that almost flattened me.

"Mine too," Dad said. He hugged me, kissed me, and then kissed my mom.

For once, being in the middle was okay. Great, in fact. I was squashed, but visible.

"You know, I'll bet you're going to be a world-famous writer someday — especially if you improve your attitude to your school work," Dad said.

My mom ran her fingers through her long hair. "Well, she ought to be," she said. "After all, she's named for Nellie McClung. And *Sowing Seeds In Danny* did sell a hundred thousand copies way back in 1908. That ought to count for something."

"Is her name spelled with a *y* or *ie*?" I asked.

"An *ie*," Mom said.

"Maybe I'll add an *ie* to my name," I said.

Dad groaned. "Oh Lord," he said. "Not another one. Women!"

We all laughed and hugged each other some more.

But I was serious. Actually, I was thinking I might even drop the hyphen and the *Harris* so my name could be in bigger letters on the cover of my books. But I didn't want to tell Mom that in case it hurt her feelings.

Second Sight

It's the television news broadcaster Victoria Calder who leads the way into our living room and invites us to sit down.

This is the woman who is slated to be the next Barbara Frum or Walters. There aren't any cameras or bars of bright lights, but we've been uptight ever since her brief phone call almost three hours ago. Victoria Calder is a woman who cannot stop falling in love.

"Mom?"

Yes, her voice is husky.

"Remember the way I used to bug you about how you knew it was true love with Dad?"

I looked at Artie. She has a new opening.

"Dad? You remember Mom always said she just *knew*. And how I thought I did too when I got married to John?"

Vickie on Artie's arm, a triumphant smile at me through her white lace veil as they pass. Her *Gone With The Wind* gown, the underwired bra built into the bodice almost popping her breasts out of the deep oval neckline, a mile-long lace train sweeping behind her. An heirloom dress granddaughters might have worn some day and she gave it to the Globe Theatre.

But Vickie is a local television personality now. She is Victoria Calder, using my first name as her professional last name. Our bride has come a long way since she followed six attendants in antebellum-style dresses down the aisle. Girls who wore makeup colour-coded to the bride's, the same no-smear blue mascara and mauve gloss lipstick. Girls who wept at her wedding and became the women who got roaring drunk at her divorce party. Our Vickie is a career woman with a media lifestyle who only has time for childless relationships. Someday I'll tell her if the pill had been around the first year Artie and I were married she would be a second-hand Austin car.

"Mom? Dad? Are you listening? You were right, Mom. When you're truly in love you just *know*! There are the usual complications, but I've fallen in love for the last time. I just know it. And I want you to be as happy as I am that it's finally happened."

Then why does the way Victoria Calder is looking at us make me think of Vickie Seitz that Christmas morning she found the goldfish Santa left for her floating belly-up in the bowl?

Suddenly Vickie's face crumples and she's sobbing into her trembling hands, head bent forward over her raised knees, curled so far over herself she's almost falling off the love seat. She has hurt herself.

Vickie has hurt herself badly. And she's all alone down there at the far end of the living room.

Artie and I stay put in our tub chairs, silent as stone pillows. We sit here to read the newspaper and watch Victoria Calder on the TV news at six. The news is always bad. Tonight is no different. Vickie needs help. She's crying the makeup off her face before asking to move home until she gets her act together.

What are we supposed to say? Do? She isn't a little girl any more. Artie and I can't take her hands and dance her around in a circle, singing

> It's love, it's love
> that makes the world go
> round
> and round
> and round
> till we all fall down!

What are we supposed to do? Say? Victoria Calder is a woman who must have an audience. It isn't Vickie Seitz who repossesses her bedroom, our lives. She'll put us through endless late night sessions of listening to her analyze herself and her new true love. We'll have to try not to look tired, bored, or to blush when she tells us why they're so great in bed together.

Snapping off the TV set won't answer anything.

"Dad? Mom?"

She's not wearing no-smear mascara.

"You'll like him. He's our new current affairs producer. From Toronto. His name's Cinch Abel."

Cinch? Of course. Current affairs.

"Honestly, you'll love him too. He's such a sensitive person. He really understands my needs. We work so well together. He wants me to host an hour-long national program on lifestyles and issues that concern the under-forty age group."

Artie's eyes close, but I know he hasn't dozed off.

"Mom? Dad? Want to meet him now? He's waiting outside in the TV station's van, probably freezing his buns off. The heater doesn't work worth a shit."

"No!" Artie and I say in unison.

Let him freeze his buns off and whatever you call his front end equipment too. Keep him on ice. I can't foresee a time when we'll ever want to meet this one.

Victoria Calder stands at our open front door to fasten the hood of her new wolf coat. There's a blizzard and the wind is whipping snow in on our new wool carpet.

"Please, don't worry. Cinch is taking me to a motel for the weekend so we can think things out. Poor Keith isn't taking it too well and neither is Cinch's ex-love."

Ex-love. Sounds like a laxative.

"I won't be back with my things until Monday. It'll be fun to be home again for a while."

We are kissed. Hugged. That was the good news? That Victoria Calder is moving in with us? Artie and I have three nights to gather our strength with some noisy love-making, to let the bad news grow stale, to despair over a daughter who cannot seem to find her one true love and settle down.

Thank God she doesn't have children now. That's the good news. That's the up-beat item to end tonight's live broadcast and it hasn't even been mentioned. The weather is a disaster.

And we've got to go out. I wouldn't mind going right to bed and crying my eyes out instead. Artie looks as if he'd like to kick something, probably the TV. Hassles about Vickie's love life leave us drained, guilt ridden.

The streets are treacherous. Artie takes one hand off the wheel and places it on my left knee. The car skids. An oncoming driver honks a warning. I put my hand over Artie's. Under these driving conditions there's no way I can let his hand creep up.

"Isn't it ironic?" Artie says. "We fell in love when we were young, got married young, had Vickie young, so we could be young grandparents. Now all we are is old parents."

Each time he says "young", and when he says "old", he squeezes my knee and I press down on his hand.

John. Keith. A few nameless ones in between. Now Cinch Abel. Why wasn't I ever able to explain to Vickie *how* I knew it was true love with Artie and not just another crush?

There was that time toward dawn on New Year's Eve. Artie and I were necking while we danced, oh so slowly, to Glenn Miller's "Sentimental Journey". As we glided across the kitchen, Artie dipped me back and there she was, her pretty wide-eyed face in front of mine, upside down. She'd heard the soft music after everyone left and sneaked downstairs to her special spying place under the breakfast nook table. We pulled her out, held her between us, danced until the record ended, and then Vickie asked her question.

"I just knew, sweetheart," I answered, "and so will you someday when your true love comes along."

Wasn't that like saying the sky is blue because it is? Will I tell our grandchildren — if we ever have any — that to some people the moon is blue cheese, but to Grandpa and me it's meringue? Isn't an answer like the one I gave Vickie an excuse for saying I don't know how I knew it was true love, I guess I just made a lucky choice?

"*Art* love strange? Calder Hilton has fallen in love at first *Seitz*!"

That's what appeared in the gossip column of our high school newspaper after I saw Artie in the Detention Room. I sent the item in myself.

Artie was in Grade 12 and I was in Grade 10. I knew I'd fallen in love when he smiled at me and my heart fluttered like a cage full of doves. But we didn't fall into each other's arms there and then.

He already had a girlfriend. And she looked a lot like me. Her friends mistook me for her sometimes and teachers often called me by her name. It made me furious. She definitely wasn't one of the Grade 11 glamour girls with so many guys on the string she wouldn't miss one. She only dated Artie. He took her to the new movie at the Cap Theatre every Friday night and they'd been seen together on Sundays at Holy Rosary Cathedral, a sure sign they were serious about each other.

Jean, my best friend, finally agreed to sneak off with me early one Sunday morning to see what went on at a Roman Catholic Mass. We sat at the back of the cathedral.

We'd heard that Catholic women wore head scarves to church instead of hats, never had time to take off their aprons, and had varicose veins that made their lisle stockings look as if they were filled with knotted ropes — a condition they suffered from because the Pope made them have too many children.

To us, the ladies who came into the cathedral didn't look any different than Anglicans or Presbyterians, although they did have more children tagging along with them.

Jean's older sister warned us we'd better not let anyone guess we weren't Catholics. She said nice Protestant girls who got caught gawking at Dogans while they worshipped their idols were turned over to the nuns to melt down for altar candles. We laughed and said we weren't going to make spectacles of ourselves.

But we got the giggles when the parade of priests walked up the middle aisle and the leader shook water on everyone from what Jean said was his wizard's wand. Our giggles got worse as we watched what the head priest did up at the altar. He swung a smoking container around as if it was too hot to handle, rang what Jean whispered was the tinkliest little fire bell she'd ever heard, and, when he washed and dried his fingers, we had to bury our faces in our coats. Every time we got our giggles under control, we would look at each other, or everyone else would suddenly sit down, or drop to their knees, and leave us standing up like plaster statues, and that would get us going again. Some of the women in front of us turned around and gave us dirty looks.

My heart flip-flopped and my giggling stopped when I saw Artie off to one side at the front. I poked Jean in the ribs and hissed at her to smarten up. He was alone. I thought that was a good sign, which it was. My prayers were answered the next day at school.

Artie was slipping out the side door as I was going back in. I'd just decided not to skip Latin any more in case he invited me to go to Mass with him sometime. He leaned against the doorjamb and asked me to the Queen City Skating Club Banquet and Dance on Saturday night.

It was a formal. Jean's sister loaned me her long dress with the black velveteen skirt and the red plaid taffeta bodice. The pink sweetheart rose corsage Artie brought me clashed, but I wore it anyway. I still have it pressed in the pages of my high school scrapbook.

We won the last spot dance, a sign if we stuck together we would have good luck, I thought. The prize was a bone china cup and saucer in a petit point rose pattern. I tucked it away in the hope chest Grandma Calder had given me when I graduated from Grade 8; it was the first thing I'd put in it.

The next weekend, Jean's sister saw Artie holding hands with his old girlfriend in the line-up outside the Cap for *To Each His Own*. She had the nerve to be mad at *me* about it. She said it had really mortified her when she tapped his girlfriend on the back and said, "Well if it isn't Calder Hilton with the guy she stole from her double," and then realized it wasn't me. I carried the Birks box down the basement to our furnace room, took the cup and saucer out of their tissue bed, and smashed them against the cement wall in the coal bin. I felt my heart cracking into a petit point pattern as I did it, but I vowed that was that for cheating Catholics.

Artie phoned me the next Friday after school. We went to see *The Best Years of Our Lives* that night, walked all the way to the Airport Inn for a Coke on Saturday, and he came to our house for the ritual roast beef dinner on Sunday night.

We were going steady.

"*But how did you know it was true love, Mom?*" I can hear Vickie asking.

I ate perogies at Artie's house without throwing up.

I hear Vickie groaning, see her rolling her eyes. Her boyfriends take her to multicultural restaurants that serve food so exotic it makes perogies sound as common as pancakes.

It was the first time I'd met Artie's parents and his brothers and sisters. Artie was always boasting about what great perogies his mom made for their Friday night suppers. I didn't have a clue what he was talking about. I thought it might be a vegetable to go with lamb chops.

Everyone sat down at the dining-room table except Artie's mother. There wasn't even a place set for her. Mrs. Seitz didn't eat dinner with us, she just served us.

At our house, after my father died, my mother sat at his end of the table to carve the meat. I took over at Mother's end and served the vegetables out of the silver entree dishes. Passing plates from one end of the table to the other to have them filled had to be done correctly. It kept us all busy until everyone was served, the blessing was said, and my mother lifted her cutlery to indicate we could take our first bite.

At Artie's house it was different. Empty plates were already set at our places when we went to the table. A blessing was said while we stood behind our chairs, the others slashed the sign of the cross on their breasts, sat down, and everyone began eating as soon as they got the food on their plates. Except me.

Mrs. Seitz leaned over my shoulder and served me first. I couldn't believe that what slid off the ladle onto my plate was cooked. It looked like half-moon pouches of raw dough.

Artie's father was seated next to me, on the side of the table farthest away from the steamy kitchen. He spooned blobs of sour cream on top of the raw dough before I could ask him to stop.

Sour cream? My mother would have flushed it down the toilet.

One of Artie's sisters laid a fork full of limp onion strings over the whole mess on my plate. I watched them sink in the thick white goo. It was white everything; table cloth, plates, food, my face. Milky white curds of cottage cheese spilled out of the perogies when I finally had to burrow down into them with my fork. Most of the family were on second helpings by then. My eyes watered every time I tried to swallow a mouthful.

"Like them? Like them?" Artie kept asking me.

I nodded my head, very slightly, afraid I might spit up what I was trying to chew and the stuff part way down my throat too.

"Mom's the best perogy maker in the world," one of Artie's brothers said.

Another brother said, "Artie ate twenty-eight of them once. He's got the record so far."

"Lots more in the kitchen. Don't be afraid to dig in," Mr. Seitz said. He smiled at me. A horrible curd was caught at his gum line over his eye-tooth.

"Mom's recipe makes a thousand," Artie said.

The napkins were just paper serviettes, too thin to hide anything. I hadn't spoken a word during the whole meal. When I finally swallowed the last bite, Mrs. Seitz asked if I'd like more. To my shock, while I held the crumpled serviette close to my mouth, I heard myself say, "Yes, please. Just a few more if you're sure you've got enough."

As Mr. Seitz reached for the bowls, I said quickly, "Without sour cream and onions, thank you. These are the most delicious perogies I've ever eaten. They don't need any garnishes."

Mrs. Seitz taught me how to make perogies the summer we decided to get married. It took us all one Friday afternoon to make the dough, roll it out, cut, fill, pinch together the edges, and stand over the pots of boiling water waiting for the egg-sized pouches to bob to the surface while we prayed none of them would come apart. My aching legs told me perogy-making probably caused more varicose veins than the Pope. I quartered the recipe and quadrupled the size of the perogies the first time I made them by myself. "Anglo-Saxon perogies" is what Artie called them because they were so big, but he said they were terrific, as good as his mother's.

My mother wasn't upset when I told her I wanted to marry Artie. She'd grown fond of him. It didn't bother her that it would be a mixed marriage. I overheard my father's older brother tell her it was a disgrace to allow me to drag a Pope-lover into the Hilton family. Mother told him to hang onto his hat because she was seeing a Roman Catholic widower who had twelve children.

We decided to elope for a lot of reasons. Mother had sold the house and she was busy getting ready to move into an apartment. We worried about how the Seitz family would get along with the Hiltons if we had a wedding and reception. Artie's father was a school janitor. My father had been a lawyer and an ORF, meaning a member of an Old Regina Family. Artie's family lived in the east end of the city, mine lived in the south end. His mother played Bingo instead of bridge. And, without my gregarious father to break the ice, Mother and Artie and I agreed we just couldn't imagine what dour Presbyterians would find to talk about with Artie's clan of devout Roman Catholics.

The five hundred dollars Mother offered us to elope was all we needed to tear up the tentative guest list. We decided to take the money and run. There was only one hitch. I had to finish my lessons in the Roman Catholic faith first.

Father O'Hara looked like an Orangeman's version of a Roman Catholic priest: too obese from rich food to be anything other than celibate, except with the nuns; dressed in a long black skirt and wearing jewellery, like a woman; blinking the bloodshot eyes of an altar wine guzzler.

Maybe he did nip at the wine. He had a flushed face with scribbles of broken blood vessels on his nose and cheeks. And there was a faint odour of sulphur about him that made me hold my breath.

Artie had to come with me to my lessons to renew his faith because he intended to marry outside the church. Father O'Hara treated him like a juvenile delinquent and called me either "chee-ild" or "Caul-dur", which sounded like Call Girl.

It made me argumentative. Was he accusing me of seducing a nice Catholic boy? Stealing him away from a good Catholic girl into a life of sin? Maybe the old geezer knew Artie's old girlfriend from hearing her confessions. I hoped so. I hoped she bored him as much as she'd bored Artie.

"I've been fitted with a diaphragm," I told Father O'Hara as I signed the pledge to bring up Artie's children in the Roman Catholic faith. "Artie wants to buy his cousin's Austin before we have a baby."

Father O'Hara belched, glared at Artie, and crossed himself.

"I feel it's my responsibility not to get pregnant on our wedding night while I'm doing my duty as a wife," I said. "Protestant girls are taught not to leave everything up to God." I gave him my most saintly smile.

"My poor chee-ild," Father O'Hara said. "Arthur would be committing adultery to lie with a girl who uses the temple of her body for lust and fornication instead of holy procreation."

"Oh, but we'll be joined in holy matrimony," I said.

"The use of birth control, my dear Caul-dur, places a Catholic soul in mortal sin."

"But confession would —"

"Absolution would not be given. Never! The sacraments would be denied to such a Catholic sinner."

I looked at Artie. He crossed himself and winked at me. *I* did not have a Catholic soul to be stained with indelible sin in the line of duty.

The sun shone on our elopement day. My mother took a snapshot of us before we left for the rectory and we're both squinting in it. There were a lot better photographs of Vickie and John that never made it into their seven-hundred-dollar wedding album.

Father O'Hara had to recruit two altar ladies from the cathedral to act as our witnesses. He'd forgotten to tell us to bring some. I don't think the ladies approved of mixed marriages that couldn't be held in the cathedral with a proper High Mass and Communion. Father O'Hara assured them I'd taken all the necessary lessons and signed the pledge. They were sniffy, but willing to suffer it through for his sake.

It was a brief ceremony. Father O'Hara kept his eyes shut through most of it, the missal open in one hand, his other hand fingering the large jewelled cross that hung down on his belly. *Damn Vatican's richer than any country in the world*, I heard my uncle say. Father O'Hara dropped the cross to put his spongy fingers over his thick lips and catch some tiny burps.

Sunshine! Man and wife! Married! A permanent state. Till death do us part. I believed it. I was Mrs. Arthur Seitz for the rest of my life and would never again be just plain Calder Hilton.

"Do you think we've done the right thing?" I asked Artie.

"Want to go back and ask Father for an annulment?"

We had our first smushy kiss as a married couple.

"Lots more in the kitchen where that came from," Artie said, holding the door of his cousin's Austin open for me. "Let's head for the lake and get to bed early."

We looked at our watches. It was 10:30 a.m. on the Monday morning we became man and wife. Consummation was a two-hour drive down a dusty gravel highway.

"Shit!" I put my hand over my mouth. What kind of married lady used words like that? "I mean, shoot! Oh, shoot, Artie. I don't have the cottage keys. I forgot to get them from Mother."

"Shall we turn back, or break in?" Artie asked.

"Break in," we said in unison.

And that's what we did. Artie shoved me through the small window over the coal oil stove and I unhooked the front door for him.

Our wedding night! Our wedding afternoon, night, and morning. The wondrous hours of shy discoveries I've never even hinted about to Vickie. I'm sure Vickie doesn't like to think her parents ever *do it*, anyway, in spite of the casual way she talks about sex. I don't think she would be surprised to learn we never went all the way before we got married.

Artie was the cuddliest thing I'd ever seen in his new blue and white striped flannelette pyjamas. He gazed at me in my silk-jersey nightie as if the Virgin Mary had appeared before him and was slowly transforming herself into Lady Chatterley.

We were both virgins so it wasn't the greatest time we've ever spent in bed. But we knew it didn't have to be. We had the rest of our lives to get better at it.

To this day, Artie and I seldom start out naked. It has nothing to do with being self-conscious about our aging bodies. We both need glasses to see anything clearly now anyway. We aren't making some sort of statement against sex scenes on *Dallas*, *Dynasty*, or the daytime soaps. We never watch any of them. It's just that we've learned it's usually more satisfying to start by unwrapping each other: peeling warm night clothes off shoulders, soft upper arms, elbows, wrists, and over groping hands, down hard and soft bellies, lean and plump hips, taut and jiggly thighs.

After thirty-five years we ought to know what's most exciting for us.

I know, I know, Victoria Calder thinks I look like any old wife and mother, so that's what I am. *Just* a housewife, menopausal hairstyle brushed up and back off my face, greying unevenly, a broken-ended perm that always seems to be almost grown out; bifocals hanging on a black cord bumping about on my Henny Penny breast when I'm not reading a recipe; my only make-up a smeary flame-red lipstick, if I remember to put it on. She thinks I get my thrills making batches of perogies or shopping at D'Allaird's for a new dress and having lunch with the girls afterwards.

And Artie? Victoria Calder tells him he looks too much like a senior civil servant, which he is. She wants him to buy designer jeans or cords to wear to the office. Artie is a man with a squeegee-clean face, no beard or moustache, who keeps his white hair trimmed short, flosses his teeth morning, noon and night, dresses in navy blue three-piece suits and polishes his black shoes every day.

Victoria Calder has been blinded by bars of bright lights and she can't see through us.

She can't see that I am Scarlett O'Hara and Artie is Rhett Butler; he is Spencer Tracy and I am Katharine Hepburn; we are Kathleen Turner and Michael Douglas, romancing. Our true love is shouting matches and angry silences because, making up after our first bad fight, we agreed we'd never divorce each other, but we didn't rule out murder. It is laughing at each other's corny jokes, witty repartee exchanged after the party is over, and widening our side of a path through a jungle of contradictions so there's room for two adventurers. And it's a tangerine tent pitched on a steep hill that can't be torn down by a breeze or a hurricane.

True love is a permanent relationship, come hell or high water. It's rituals I've never told Vickie about, like the Pillow Slip War.

Once a week, Artie and I stand at our sides of the bed, our pillows on it in front of us, clean folded pillow slips lying on top of them. We are tense, on the mark, ready, set — go! The one who gets the pillow into its slip first is the winner, the Night of Clean Sheets Aggressor. This housewife is deft at putting on pillow slips swiftly.

"But how did you know it was true love, Mom? How did you just know?" the voice of Vickie Seitz echoes.

I can't find the answer for Victoria Calder or for our Vickie Seitz, hidden deep in that television personality.

But I can sit down beside my daughter on the love seat and listen to what she says, to how she feels.

Maybe she'll want to listen to me, too. I might get up the nerve to tell her my heart still skips a beat when I catch sight of her father unexpectedly somewhere. It happened the other day in the mall, I'll tell her. I'd just tucked a few more U.S. dollars into our winter getaway account and was going up the escalator to see what was on sale at D'Allaird's when I saw Artie coming out of Sears. My heart did the same old flippity-flop. And, mad as I am about the money he spent on an energy-efficient furnace when we could just go south to keep warm, my heart knows the truth. The next time the sight of Artie takes me by surprise, it will act up the same way.

That's how I know it's true love. It has nothing to do with common sense. Vickie may experience some other more modern sign. But, if she knows, just *knows*, she has found her one true love at last, Artie and I will be happy to meet Cinch Abel.

It could be a good sign that his name is so easy to remember.

II

Webs

The Lookout Stone

Going out of the valley, coming in, nothing is supposed to be hidden from view up here. This rock is a special watching place on the hills around our old family cottage. It doesn't change. The yellow patches of lichen that roughen the bone-white surface, and the hollow footholds, one a step ahead of the other, still make it possible to sit here without sliding off down the steep slope.

I'm glad to sit down, catch my breath. How can the valley look so shallow, so much closer, and the climb to the Lookout Stone seem so difficult now? Age. Tension. Too many cigarettes. Even three ultralights a day are too many. But this fourth one's a bonus, good medicine to ease the stress of waiting for Jean and anticipating our annual Victoria Day weekend fight about getting rid of the lake property.

Last year she started the fireworks long before it was time to reward ourselves with a gin and tonic.

"Face facts, Prentice," Jean began. That's her ritual opening, the implication being that she's the practical sister. "What's the point in coming all the way back here each May just to clean and close the place up again? We're stupid not to sell, you know that."

We were down on our knees in our traditional face-off at the carefully measured dead centre of the thirty-foot living room, ready to begin washing the oiled floorboards. Neither of us ever wanted to do more than our fair share, so we start there, head-to-head in the middle, and back away from each other to the end walls. My special cleansing solution of lake water, Lysol and melted shavings of Sunlight soap waited in dented galvanized pails beside each of us. The solution loses some of its pleasant medicated odour of hospitals and healing if it gets cold. Jean knows I like to work fast. A musty smell like dead leaves in a compost heap lingers in the cottage until the floor is done.

"One-two-three . . . scrub!" I said, dipping my scrub brush into my pail, slapping it to the floor, and rubbing it back and forth furiously.

Jean sat back on her haunches. She had her scrub brush in one hand and her half of the old towel we'd torn apart in the other hand, both dry as dust. "It's idiotic to hang on and on. Why should we make these soppy sentimental journeys each year to be cleaning women?"

I flopped my rag onto the floor to mop up the excess water and wrung it into my pail. Her argument always follows the same well-rehearsed pattern of reasonable statements alternating with reasonable questions. At least that's her opinion.

"Scrub!" I said. "I plan on retiring here someday."

She snorted and dropped her brush and rag into her pail with a splash that caused the solution to spill out and make pools on the floor. "Instead of Victoria? You're going to choose a prairie coulee over paradise island?"

"The Qu'Appelle Valley isn't a coulee," I said.

"You would do that, Prentice. When are you going to face facts? This place isn't even winterized."

"I'll insulate, put in electric or propane heat, add a rug or two. It's the only family property we have and I think we ought to hang onto it."

"Some family property. Ohh . . . memories are made of this, aren't they? Holidays spent on our knees."

"And hands," I told her, "on our hands and our knees. Scrub! You're breaking the rules. I've made arrangements to leave my share to our kids and I know you'll leave yours to Cindy."

"I'll what? To who?" She leaned forward and glared at me.

I kept my voice low, even though I'd scrubbed and mopped my way quite a distance from her. "Look, Jean, none of my kids are perfect either. It's time you stopped acting as if Cindy's dead and buried just because she's living with a poet on Saltspring Island."

"Shut up! Tell it to someone who cares." Jean plunged her hand into her pail, grabbed the sodden floor rag, and threw it at me.

I caught it and tossed it back into her pail. Then I finished my half of the floor without saying another word. She was finally scrubbing her half as if she could erase it when I left to climb up here, to the Lookout Stone.

This year, if she's changed her mind again and decided to make the trip from Calgary after all, I'll bring her up here to see, really see, the Qu'Appelle Valley. I'll tell her how once, after Mr. Martell finished digging a new hole for our biffy and I was keeping him company while he rolled and smoked a cigarette, he told me this rock was a teardrop left by his ancestors on the brow of Old Buffalo Back Hill.

"So's the people that's strong an not scared got a place to see in four directions," he said, pinching the paper at one end and licking his bottom lip so the cigarette would stick there while he talked. "Them spirits speak loud, girl. Dreams'll come round. An youse gotta be strong for it. Real strong."

I nodded as if I knew what he meant. We were sitting side by side, leaning back against the mound of earth beside the new hole. I liked the slow way Mr. Martell talked, the silences he left after each thing he said, and I liked the smell of his cigarette smoke mixed with the scent of the moist loam and clay behind us. Mr. Martell's arms reminded me of the dry branches that broke off our ash trees when the breeze was so light the poplars were just clapping their leaves politely. He didn't look strong enough to dig a six-foot hole. But people who ice-fished at Katepwa told how he often climbed to the Lookout Stone, quick as a deer, and sat here for hours, even if it was twenty below with a bad wind.

In the summers, I sat here a lot. I was the first one to see my father coming into the valley on Friday nights and the last to see him going out on Sunday nights. Sometimes Mr. Martell came out of his house on the edge of No Man's Land and raised his arm toward me in greeting. I waved back in a beckoning manner, but, after a few moments, he always lowered his arm and turned away. Everything is different down there now. His two-storey house was hauled away years ago to make room for that private tennis court. Fancy summer homes line the shore of No Man's Land in front of where the whitewashed Laroche cabins once huddled together. Steel-link fences with three strands of barbed wire strung along the top protect the properties of the new summer people. Poodles yip behind padlocked gates. I miss the baying of the coyote mutts the Laroche families kept.

Changes come and go in a circle around this rock. Bubbles of cactus, still covered with lace shrouds of last year's needles, are beginning new networks of sharp pointed barbs to spear the sun. Tiger lilies are sprouting from roots warmed under Old Buffalo Back's hide to flame briefly in July. Summer is starting its semi-circle of expected surprises. Nothing will happen for the last time, or for the first time, here, as it did on that Victoria Day weekend seven months after my father died.

Mother had promised we would open the cottage as usual — as usual, except she wanted to wait until Saturday morning to drive to the valley.

Bruce and I packed the car for her on Friday night. We didn't fight. He called me "Sis" instead of "Fang Face" and I called him "Kid" instead of "Brat". We said "excuse me" to each other. Even Jean behaved nicely, skipping back and forth to the car carrying small things for us without whining. Everyone was cheerful. But long after we had some cocoa and said our goodnights, I heard Mother crying softly again in bed.

She didn't do that often, only before *firsts*: Dad's forty-eighth birthday (ten days after his fatal coronary thrombosis); Christmas Eve; my eighteenth birthday in January; Valentine's night; and on a few nights when I didn't know what she was going to have to get through for the first time on her own. The sound of my mother's muffled sobs always made me cry too. When she stopped crying and I was finally able to fall asleep, I would dream my father was really still alive, but, for some reason he hadn't explained, it was a secret I had to keep.

I would wake up in those dreams, go outside, and find my father in his garden of Qu'Appelle Valley plants he had moved to our backyard in Regina. Striding around making a pie in the snow was how I'd found him when the dreams began before his birthday in November. Later, when spring came, he was squishing through the wet crested wheatgrass, stopping to inspect his plants and shrubs for the first signs of green shoots or buds. I walked beside him, circling the garden with him, not a bit cold in my pyjamas and bare feet. We talked about things that had happened since he'd gone away. It was just as if he had come back from a medical meeting in Winnipeg or Saskatoon and I was the first one to welcome him home. I kept forgetting to tell him Mother had been crying.

Everything went wrong in the dream I had that Friday night in May before we opened the cottage without him.

My father was sitting in a wheelchair with his back toward me when I came out of the house. He was outside of his garden, parked in front of the archway he'd built as an entrance into it. The back door slammed shut behind me, but the noise didn't attract his attention. It was very cold, so cold the step seemed to be iced, and my feet stuck to it as my tongue once had on the metal flagpole at school.

"Hi, Dad. Dad? Hey! You're not going to try and get through that dumb arch in that stupid wheelchair, are you?" My voice got louder with each word, and gusts of wind whipped my frozen breath up to Mother's bedroom window, where each puff shattered against the glass like sleet. She would wake up and start crying again.

"Hey Dad, it's the first weekend of summer. Remember? What's going on?" I kept my voice down to a stage whisper.

My father didn't move, didn't turn around or speak.

"It's all your fault," I said. "You can't get through sitting in that stupid thing." The tete-a-tete benches he'd built inside the trellis arch were too close together. It was a family joke. The anatomy of archways eluded him, he used to say. I wanted to say something funny about how he had misread his own carefully drawn plans and hear him laugh about it again, but I just kept repeating, "Your fault, your fault. Fault. Fault. Fault."

"What?" he exclaimed. "What the hell's bells?" He still didn't turn or (I was waiting for it) jump out of the wheelchair with a whoop to grab me and dance me through the arch — as if I was Ginger Rogers and he was Fred Astaire. We weren't going to trip the light fantastic around his garden to celebrate the beginning of summer.

"A good doctor wouldn't have done it," I yelled, and watched my words order themselves into a sign across the top of the archway. Each letter was formed of frozen droplets of spit that winked like tiny Christmas tree bulbs.

"What? What-what-what?" My father turned to face me. He was smiling the way he did when I forgot the punch line of a joke.

The soles of my feet burned with pain as I pulled them off the iced step and walked toward him. "Don't you mean, 'I beg your pardon,' Father?" I slid by him and went through the archway into his garden, hoping he would get out of the ugly chair and follow me. I circled his garden, dancing lightly on my toes from plant to plant, touching a budding branch or a green shoot before twirling and going on to the next one. He had been so careful transplanting each one from the valley loam to city gumbo — chokecherry and saskatoon bushes, cactus, and, next to neatly-labelled stakes, tiger lilies, brown-eyed susans, wild snapdragons we called scrambled eggs, and a weed he was sure was going to turn out to be ditch daisies.

I spun back out through the archway like a dust-devil and stopped in front of him. "Your garden's going to be a mess unless you stick around and show me how to look after it. Everything will die," I said.

"Yes," he said, "everything does. In the meantime, errors of commission are regarded with tolerance and understanding. Errors of omission are inexcusable."

"But you omitted to live!" I shouted.

Suddenly, his head lolled forward and his mouth sagged open. The flesh began melting off his face and drooling down his chin onto his chest.

"Stop it! Stop it!" I screamed. "You can't be like that. Not ever. Not dead — dying. Stop joking. It's not funny." I knelt down and tried to shake the wheelchair, sobbing and saying, "Listen, Daddy, it's okay. It's okay if you're in a wheelchair. We don't care if you're crippled. Please Daddy, please stop it. Wake up — wake up — wake . . ."

I awoke from that dream hanging onto the cold radiator beside my bed, trying to shake it. Spittle was running down my chin. Something had gone wrong. I had awakened too soon. The dream wasn't over. It couldn't be. I had to go back to sleep, fix up the ending, wake up knowing I could coax him to come back in another dream and everything would be the same again. But I knew it was too late. Something had changed, ended.

Gradually, over the thirty-four years since that last dream, the view from this Lookout Stone has changed, like much in my life. The pit in the Little Lime Hill, where we dumped our tin cans and broken glass for so many years, has been filled and sealed with cement. Matching blue Lincolns belonging to the professional couple who bought the property are parked on its flat paved top between a pair of brass coach lamps. A luminous sign on the stone gatepost says, PRIVATE PROPERTY — TRESPASSERS WILL BE PROSECUTED. Mother Bunting, the hill to the north of me, has sagged until her nipple no longer seems to rub the sky. In front of her, the scars left by motorcycles and snowmobiles on Baby Bunting Hill are ripe and raw in the sun. But if I look off to the south, beyond the end of the lake to the double arches of the cement bridge on the old road coming into the valley, no time has passed up here.

I can see Mother gripping the steering wheel of the new '49 Chev as we reach the foot of Corkscrew Hill and approach the rickety cow bridge over Skinner's Creek. Her knuckles are white. Dad always patted the Green Hornet's dashboard and honked the old '37 Chev's horn when we made it safely across the bridge without it caving in. "You're a great old crate," he would say, winking at Mother. "I may never trade you in." But he did, and died before he could drive the new car into the valley.

Mother drove slowly, squinting into the morning sun. She had cried a long time the night before and her eyelids were pink and puffy. We didn't chant the usual refrain to celebrate the beginning of summer when we saw the lake, but I could hear the echo of our voices:

> May the Twenty-fourth is
> the Queen's birthday.
> If we don't get a holiday,
> we'll all run away.

Running wasn't what we were doing. We crept along the valley road. And I knew Mother had been right to wait until daytime. Opening the cottage at night without him would have been worse. Darkness

THE LOOKOUT STONE 77

everywhere. Closed shutters. Padlocked doors. Only damp matches in a tin up on a shelf too high to reach to light the oil lamps and cookstove. Making our beds with flannelette slabs wintered in the black bedding box Dad had built. No. Bruce and I had known better than to even discuss it with Mother. This trip could only be almost the same, not the way it had been when he brought us down to open the cottage.

Mother stepped on the gas on the straight stretch of road before the cement bridge. The speedometer needle went up to the speed limit of forty-five.

Yes, I thought, let's get it over with.

Bruce dropped his Batman comic book on the back seat beside him and leaned forward, grinning. "You gonna honk the horn now, Mom? I'll show you how." He hit the back of the seat with his fist and said, "Honk! Honk! Honk-honk!"

"Hip! Hip! Hoo-ray!" Jean yelled, bouncing up on the seat between Mother and me to see how close we were to the cottage.

Jean was right. Dad's honking always sounded like a cheer, especially from the Lookout Stone. Mother honked, but it was different. It wasn't just the new car, a sleek grey ghost compared to the Green Hornet, the bitter smell of some car salesman's cigar smoke still caught in its upholstery. The rhythm was wrong. The sound was slow and heavy.

"So young — so young — so young," everyone said when my father died. That had sounded wrong to me then too. I thought it described someone like David Thompson, a boy I'd been secretly in love with who'd died when he was in Grade 11 and I was in Grade 9. David was buried just a few days before his seventeenth birthday, not his forty-eighth. I didn't think "so young" applied to my father. After all, I was grown up — almost eighteen, his hair was getting grey, and he'd had a heart attack. But he was a doctor, and I just couldn't believe a doctor would let himself die.

At first it seemed dramatic and exciting when Uncle Fred, my father's older brother, came to get me at Reliance Business School. The principal ushered him into the classroom in the middle of a shorthand exam she was giving us. I could see why my parents called him The Deacon. Uncle Fred walked with his eyes cast heavenwards and he didn't seem to approve of what he saw up there. He put his hand on my shoulder. "Your father is gravely ill," he said. His voice was hushed, but everybody in the room heard him. "Your mother asked me to bring you home."

I got up and followed him down the aisle to the door. I left the exam papers and my stenographer's notebook on my desk. A good secretary wouldn't leave a mess like that, I thought, I'll flunk shorthand and office deportment.

"Is my father sick enough to die?" I asked Uncle Fred as soon as we were outside. I was recalling deathbed scenes in novels where family members stood around the dying person's bed, saying interesting things about life. I couldn't remember what. The favourite daughter usually vowed to fulfill some goal her dying parent had set for her. I thought I could tell my father that I'd changed my mind and did want to go to university after all. I stepped on Uncle Fred's heels and asked again, "Is Daddy dying, Uncle Fred?"

"Your father is gravely ill, Prentice," he repeated. "We don't have any time to waste talking about it."

Our front door was never locked, but that day Uncle Fred's wife, Aunt Ivy, was there holding it open. I wondered why she wasn't upstairs with the others, around his bed, and then I remembered those deathbed scenes always ended with someone really dying. Aunt Ivy threw her flowered silk arms around me. I managed to struggle free.

"How's Daddy?" I asked.

"He's fine now, darling, just fine." Aunt Ivy sighed and patted my cheek.

That was when I started to shake. I ran through the vestibule, the front hall, and got half-way up the stairs to my parents' bedroom before I stumbled and had to sit down. He's just fine, I thought. Thank you, God. Everything is okay. How do you write "okay" in shorthand? I put my head down and sobbed with relief.

"Prentice, oh, Prentice. Go ahead. Cry, dear." My mother was kneeling on the stairs in front of me, stroking my hair. "It was very quick, dear," she said. "He didn't suffer before he died."

"He died? Died?"

Mother hugged me.

"Is he dead?" I asked.

"Yes, dear," Mother answered softly.

I looked down at Aunt Ivy, who was standing at the foot of the stairs, hugging herself and sighing. Mother turned and looked at her too. "She's a liar," I said. "Why did she say Daddy was fine?" If my mother answered, I didn't hear her over my sobs.

I tried to avoid my aunt during the next few days. It wasn't easy. She was everywhere, and I thought it looked as if she was enjoying herself, although I didn't see her smile once.

Mother seemed to be smiling all the time. She met people at the door with a smile, and she led the laughter after anecdotes they told about funny things my father had said or done on the golf course, at the poker table, and at medical meetings. Mother smiled when she told them my father liked to consider himself a natural born carpenter. She said he'd designed a secret compartment for the new library desk at the cancer clinic, and helped the cabinet-maker install it, so that nobody, including her, had been able to find it. A murmur of "so young" followed some of the stories, almost like a forgotten punch line. The unspoken words were there under my mother's tinkling laughter, and Aunt Ivy's somber offerings of tea, coffee, or — said with her customary sigh and a scowl — something stronger if she could find it. Scotch and rye whiskey and sherry were all out in plain view on the kitchen table.

There wasn't any company for Mother to smile for before the funeral. We had the living room all to ourselves as we waited for the limousine to pick us up and take us to the church.

"You know what I'm going to do?" Jean said. "I'm going to rap on the glass of Daddy's coffin and tell him to sing 'Cruising Down The River' with me."

Mother stopped pacing back and forth in front of her upholstered rocker that faced my father's empty easy chair, and sat down in it. "Well, we aren't going to sing that song today, dear," Mother said, motioning for Jean to get on her lap. She smiled. "It's a bit too cheerful, sweetheart. We'll sing 'Unto The Hills Beyond' instead. You'll like it too, Jean-bean. It was one of your daddy's favourite psalms."

Bruce sat down in Dad's chair and crossed his legs. "His coffin's oak, anyway, not glass. Dad loved good wood."

"It's glass!" Jean screamed. "So shut up!"

"Hush, Jean-bean. No it isn't, Bruce is right," Mother said. "What on earth gave you the idea it was glass, dear?"

"Daddy said Snow White had a glass coffin," Jean said, and she began crying. She stopped when Mother laughed.

"Snow White? Snow White?" Mother laughed as she had when the visitors were there, in crescendos, the way she laughed at cocktail parties to fill awkward silences.

The same way we all laughed while we were opening the cottage that May. Bruce was so proud that he'd remembered to bring a pocketful of dry Eddy matches. One by one, he broke them, snapping the heads off as he tried to strike them on the seat of his pants to light the cookstove, the way Dad always did. Bruce started to cry, soundlessly, and ran out of the cottage. We just stood there, cold and shivering. The cottage was like a tomb. I went out to find Bruce and climbed up here to the Lookout Stone.

That time, I didn't sit down. I stood on this rock poised like an Olympic torch bearer. I was a statue, one foot ahead of the other in the footholds, my right arm held aloft, my hand a fist clenched around nothing. What was I thinking then? *Citius, Altius, Fortius*: Faster,

Higher, Braver? Perhaps. I was proud of my B-plus in Grade 12 Latin. I liked the idea of being able to translate a dead language into a living one.

I must have known the Olympic creed, too. The 1948 Games were one of my father's favourite topics in his last summer. Yes, I knew the creed: "Not to win, but to take part; not the triumph, but the struggle; not to have conquered, but to have fought well." But I didn't believe it, not then, standing on this stone with the last dream of my father circling away. I leapt off the Lookout Stone at a run, going faster and faster down the steep slope until I believed — I knew — that if the next step didn't split me in half, I would fly across the valley. I would soar to the top of Beacon Point Hill, and higher, higher. For one long stride, the valley was forgotten. My body and mind stretched up together and I was airborne before I fell. The scraping and tumbling ended in the wound where Old Buffalo Back's hide had been torn away to get at a vein of gravel.

I didn't move. I cursed my father for letting himself die, Aunt Ivy for the false hope she held out to me, and Mr. Martell too, for not teaching me how to see in four directions.

Bruce found me lying there, my mouth full of sand, and we went back to the cottage together without speaking.

Now, I'm up here on the Lookout Stone waiting for Jean, and, at the same time, I'm down on the grassy slope in front of our cottage, carrying things down from the new car, watching Bruce help Mother find the right keys for the padlocks. Jean is skipping back and forth singing "Cruising Down The River", getting in everyone's way, and she's sitting at the wheel of her Mercedes, listening to jazz on her tape deck, planning the questions and statements she'll use to make me face facts, at last. Mother is telling Bruce it's okay, she can open the cottage alone, and she's laughing in trills at a bridge table in Sunny View Lodge so no one will suspect she's uncertain which card to play next. We are all so young and scared down there. I'm carrying my father's medical bag into the cold cottage, an eighteen-year-old dreamer who is telling herself it's the glare from the lake that's making her eyes water.

My vision is blurred by the wind that brushes the brow of Old Buffalo Back Hill. I look south toward the cement bridge with its curved arches, and I see my father coming into the valley. I hear the horn of the old Green Hornet: Hip! Hip! Hoo-ray! And I wonder how a father who isn't quite forty-eight will greet a daughter who is four years older than he is. What will it be like to talk to my father now? Will we laugh or cry or be as silent as death?

As the car gets closer, honking my father's signal, I'm not disappointed to see it's my sister's green Mercedes. I'm ready to go. I tuck my package of cigarettes under the back of the Lookout Stone and begin picking my way carefully down the steep slope.

Aunt Hobby

It's easy to see Aunt Hobby is in her Aunt Hideous mood when she arrives at the lake with Grandma for their annual holiday. She refuses to get out of the car.

Mother opens the car door for her, leans in, and kisses her on the cheek, the cheek with the huge mole on it that has hair growing out of it. "Come on, Hazel dear," she says. "We're so glad you could come. A week out here in the fresh air is just what you need."

Aunt Hobby doesn't budge. Her big brown oxfords are planted on the rubber floor mat, toes turned out, heels wide apart and dug down. She has her arms locked around the tapestry handiwork bag on her lap, thick fingers fastened along her hairy forearms, and that awful not-budging grin on her face. That's the grin she had last summer when she sat on my brother and almost squashed him to death because he was teasing her. My brother and I have been told to be especially patient and considerate of her this summer. She's been in the hospital again. I'm not supposed to know why, but I do. She tried to kill herself. I'd like to see if she has scars on her wrists from her embroidery scissors. That's what she used just a couple of weeks ago. But Aunt Hobby's wrists are hidden and she's not moving a muscle.

Grandma sighs and says to leave her be, she'll get out of the car when she's ready. So Aunt Hobby just sits there, stiff as a corpse, all afternoon. My brother and I are building a fort in the bushes so we can hide from her when we think she's getting dangerous. Every once in a while she makes us jump by shouting out another complaint against Grandma:

"Mother? That ride wasn't as long as you promised!

"You didn't go both ways past the pool hall on Main Street, Mother!

"You knew I wanted to go by the playground and wave good-bye to my little friends. So why didn't you do it, stupid?"

My brother and I look at each other. Aunt Hobby never made any friends because she was too slow to go to school. Kids always taunt her, and follow her sometimes, hulking along the sidewalk the way she does, grunting and talking to themselves about men at the pool hall, and then they tear off into the bushes giggling when Aunt Hobby turns around.

At tea time, Mother calls us in and asks if we'll go and tell Aunt Hobby a cup is poured for her. We do, and she just slams the car door in our faces.

When we're sent out at supper time to ask her to come in and eat, she rolls down the window and shouts, "Tell stupid I want to go for a car ride and see my boyfriends." Grandma fixes her plate and covers it with one of the tea towels Aunt Hobby cross-stitched.

It begins to look like Aunt Hobby is going to spend the night in the car. But she's afraid of the dark. So am I when she's around. Just before it's time to light the lamps, I'm sent out to coax her inside. Mother and Grandma are busy stringing blankets across one end of the veranda to make the private sleeping place that Grandma always shares with Aunt Hobby. I don't want to go. I hesitate for so long my brother thinks he's going to have to go and he hands me his flashlight.

I shine the flashlight into the car and rap on the window. "I've got some new books," I tell her. "I'll let you read one of them if you'll come in now."

She grunts.

"A brand new Dorothy Dix and the new Nancy Drew. You can have first pick."

She scowls.

"The Nancy Drew one is *The Clue of the Tapping Heels*. It starts out really good. Nancy makes up this secret code she taps out with her feet. I've read the first chapter, but I'll let you have that one if you want."

She opens the car door, heaves herself out, snatches the flashlight out of my hand, and drops it into her handiwork bag.

"Hey! That's my brother's," I say. "Give that back."

The long low growl she makes when she's really angry is her only reply. I can practically feel the earth shake as she marches off toward the cottage. I follow. I hate the short-sleeved cotton dresses she sews for herself and their horrible floral prints. Her arms look like prehistoric lizards lying along the edges of a big flower bed.

Aunt Hideous goes right to the cheese box beside my camp cot, picks up both of my new books and *Maida's Little Shop*, one of my very favourites I read every summer, and drops them into her bag.

"Hey! You can't take all of them," I say.

She glares straight ahead of her, brushes me aside, and goes out of the cottage. I'm right behind her.

Half-way down the steps to the shore, she turns around and shoves me off the path. I land on my backside in the thistles and wild rose bushes with the breath almost knocked out of me. I get to the shore just as she's throwing my books into the water.

"There!" she says. "Fetch!"

"Hey! What do you think you're doing?" I try to get a deep enough breath to shout for Mother and Grandma.

Then she hauls the flashlight out of her bag, turns it off, and throws it into the lake too.

"Go fetch, stupid! Fetch them!" she snarls at me.

While my mother is putting Mercurochrome on my scratches, I ask her what's the matter with Aunt Hobby.

She just sighs. I ask again.

"Hazel lost her temper," she says. "It's frustrating for her sometimes. She doesn't like herself."

"How old is she anyway?" The cold glass dropper stops moving down the back of my leg. I wait.

Mother dips the dropper into the bottle before she replies. "More than three times older than you," she says, sighing again. Sometimes I've heard my mother talking to my father about Aunt Hobby and I can tell she's crying. I'd cry too if I had a sister as ugly as that.

"Why doesn't she act her age?" I ask. "Is she crazy or something?"

"No. Hold still. Poor Hazel had measles and chicken pox and scarlet fever all together when she was six."

"Then how come she didn't die? Grandma says lots of people died just from the flu in the olden days."

"Stop wiggling," Mother says. "This isn't iodine."

"My books and the flashlight are ruined and you don't even care."

"Of course I do. Don't be silly. Hazel will buy your brother a new flashlight out of her allowance."

"What about my books? Two of them were brand new."

"Stop whining. We're almost through. Hazel brought down exactly the same books as you did with her this summer. She'll let you choose which one you want to read first and then give them to you for keeps when she goes home. She wants to make up and be friends with you.

Okay? Remember what I said about being patient and understanding with your aunt?"

The first thing Aunt Hobby wants to do is teach me how to spoolknit. She shows me how to hammer the nails in around the top of an empty spool of thread. I hold the nails and she hammers. Twice, she hits my fingers, but I don't let out a peep.

Spoolknitting is so easy I can't believe it. Aunt Hobby lets me use some small balls of wool from the bottom of her bag. We each make a hot place mat.

While we're sewing our tubes together, side by side at the long pine table, she uses her darning needle to point out where my stitches are sloppy and stabs it into my hand, drawing blood. She says she's sorry, that it was just an accident, so I don't make a fuss. I suck the wounds until they stop bleeding. Grandma says that Hazel is often clumsy, that we've got to humour her so she won't lose her temper and have to be sent away.

Mother keeps saying how lucky I am to have an aunt to teach me crafts. She says her sister is the family craftswoman, an artist. Then she admires the mat I've made.

"Ugly colours she used," Aunt Hobby says. "I hate them."

"Oh, but see, Hazel dear? See how smart they look with Mother's old Blue Willow dishes?" My mother holds the mat I made under the saucer of her tea cup. It's about the same size.

"Aunt Hobby's got enough red, white and blue wool to make you a big enough mat for under the platter," I say. "Look." I reach down into her handiwork bag and pull out three skeins.

"That wool's mine! You can't have another ounce of it!" Aunt Hobby grabs the skeins, hooks her thumbs over the wool, stretches them out tight, and glares down at them. "Ugly colours," she growls. "Too bright to even wind."

"They're a lot nicer than those ugly dark colours you used," I say, and suddenly she reaches out, pulls the skeins over my head, and begins trying to wrap the strands of wool around my neck. Her hands work furiously, her lizard arms writhing around me too fast for me to bite them to make her let go.

Mother shrieks, jumps up, and starts slapping Aunt Hobby's hands.

Grandma runs out from behind the blankets, crying, "Hazel? Hazel! Stop that at once. Let go of her. Let go of that wool right now, Hazel."

Aunt Hobby wraps her hands around my throat and growls softly, "I thought you liked my wool so much you'd want to be wound in it." Then she slowly untangles her fingers from the wool, drops her hands to her hips with a smack, and, in her little girl voice, says to

Grandma, "I was winding. She was holding." She sticks her lower lip out in the frog-pout she makes whenever Grandma gets cross with her.

Grandma sends Aunt Hobby off behind the blankets. "There now," she says to me after she's gone. "No harm done." She holds my face between her soft hands and kisses me on both cheeks. "Go fetch your brother from your fort and the three of us will have a swim."

We're floating on our backs, riding the waves, when Grandma says, "Your aunt is going through a very bad stage, I'm afraid."

"You're not kidding," my brother says. "She's a monster."

Grandma says, "She was a beautiful child. Prettier than your sister, than her sisters, too."

"She's sure ugly now." My brother rolls over and dives into a wave before Grandma can scold him.

"You know, dear," she says to me, "your aunt used to look just like you before she got sick."

I say, "I know. Mother told me that once."

"Hazel knows she's not pretty now. She's not blind, she can see in the mirror." Grandma takes my hand and we do the threshing machine backstroke together until we're a long way out in the lake. When we're floating again, she says, "The doctor says I'll have to put her in a hospital. But I'm sure I can get her violent outbursts under control by keeping her busy. The peace and quiet down here will do her a world of good if we all do our best for her."

I swear to myself that I'll be nice to Aunt Hobby if it kills me.

When we get up to the cottage after our swim, Aunt Hobby is busy knitting another pair of argyle socks for the boys overseas. Grandma calls them leggings, which is more accurate. Knitting the criss-crossing pattern fascinates my aunt so much she hates switching to plain wool when it's time to turn the heel and knit the foot. So, after going a long way past that point, she just casts off. You can tell it worries her not to do what the pattern says. Her needles stop clicking and she pulls at the hairs growing out of the mole on her cheek, counting the extra rows out loud. Everyone has to keep quiet while she's doing that or she has a tantrum.

Knitting an argyle legging keeps Aunt Hobby from causing any trouble until Grandma and Mother have our noon dinner ready. She's an angel at the table, too, saying the blessing before we eat and after we're finished.

Then Grandma tells my brother she doesn't mind waiting until he finishes clearing the table to take the laundry down to Lily at No Man's Land. She says if he gets a wiggle on, she'll let him sit on her lap and steer the car.

Aunt Hobby turns into Aunt Hideous again the minute Grandma says "car". She stamps her feet so hard the cottage shakes. She pounds the table with her fists and the dishes rattle and bounce. And she howls in that frightening way she does when she's furious.

"Hazel! Remember what I told you?" Grandma says, patting her on the back. "Friends help each other get the chores done before they can expect any treats. I promise I'll take you for a long car ride later. Down to the store for an ice cream cone if you wish. After the dishes are all dried and put away. But you have to behave like you promised."

Mother suggests playing I Spy while we're doing the dishes so it won't be so boring. Aunt Hobby won't join in. She hums in her tuneless way until I've dried almost everything. She just stands there, a platter in her hand, practically rubbing the pattern off it.

"I spy who I'm going to marry!" she yells suddenly. Her eyes are closed tight. "The Laroche twins!" She opens her eyes and grins.

"They're already married," I say, wondering if she's just pretending to be dumb to get out of her fair share of drying.

"I remember when you used to say *you* were going to marry the Laroche twins," Mother says to me, smiling as if it was a joke. She turns to look at her sister. "The twins really are married, Hazel dear."

"I don't care. They're handsomer than any of the men I've seen at the pool hall and *I'm* marrying both of them." Aunt Hobby throws her tea towel into the dishpan.

Mother lifts it out, wrings it, and hands it back to her. "Hazel dear, you can only marry one man at a time," she says.

Aunt Hobby stamps her foot. "Why? Just because that's what you and my other sisters did doesn't mean I have to. I'm different. If I go last, I get two boys to marry. I'm marrying them this summer."

She's crazy, no matter what my mother says. "The twins are away at the war," I say, testing to see just how crazy she really is. "Are you planning to go overseas to marry them?"

Her laugh is evil. "Of course not, stupid. We're getting married in the little Anglican church with its beautiful stained glass windows, and I'm wearing your mother's wedding dress. You can be my flower girl if you're good."

I give up.

Mother takes the dishpan out to empty it into the bushes. I hang my tea towel on the rack. My back is to Aunt Hobby when she snaps her wet tea towel at me and catches me just behind the knees where it really stings.

She says, "There! That'll teach you not to be mean and jealous. You're too young to get married to anybody."

The next few days are scorchers. The rest of us spend most of the time at the shore, in and out of the water, staying in the lake until we look like we need ironing when we come out, not even drying off before we go back in again.

Aunt Hobby sits in her chair on the shady side of the veranda with partially finished pieces of handiwork all around her — a rag rug she's hooking, pillow slips and a table cloth she's embroidering, an afghan she's crocheting, some lace she's tatting, and a legging.

Grandma keeps sending me up to ask her to come down to the water before she melts. Aunt Hobby isn't a pretty sight.

Her flowered dresses are always soaking wet under her arms and her heavy breasts. Sweat covers her forehead and even her mashed potato knees glisten with it. She keeps her stockings rolled down to her ankles and her legs are white as dough under the long black hair. I try to talk her into coming down to the shore and at least dabbling her feet in the water to cool off. The crayfish would eat off her toes, she says, looking down at her big brown brogues.

The first time she says that I almost laugh. But I tell her the crayfish at the shore are all dead and if she comes down there with me I'll show her how Lily makes necklaces out of crayfish claws. "It's a craft you'll like," I say. "What you do is break the little pincer parts off, clean the guck out of the big claws, wash them in soap and water, then set them in the sun for a few days so they'll get redder and lose their smell, and you string them on a ribbon with knots between them, like pearls. Lily says even wearing just one crayfish claw makes you lucky in love." I think this will get her interested, but it doesn't. She just sits there like a lump, staring at me.

The only relief Aunt Hobby gets from the sweltering heat is in the dirt cellar. She goes down there several times a day and sits on an overturned crock. That's where she is when Grandma sends me up to the cottage to mix a pitcher of lemonade for us.

"Aunt Hobby?" I call, leaning over the edge of the dark hole. It smells worse than mossy lake weeds do when they've rotted on the shore.

She grunts.

There are pale crickets down there the size of dinosaurs. "Will you please hand me up the lemonade base?" I ask.

"Come fetch it yourself, stupid," she says.

"Aw, come on," I say. "Please? I'll bring you the first glass I mix. I'm going to get fresh well water for it too."

Just another grunt, followed by a growl.

"What's the matter with you? There isn't enough room down there for both of us. Pretty please?"

She begins humming. It's never a tune I can recognize.

Before I know what I'm doing, I slam the trap door shut and stand on it.

"Arghh!" she bellows.

I hear the thud of her shoes on the ladder rungs. She's coming up to get me!

I jump off the door and run for my life.

When I get back to the shore, panting, I tell them the well's dry and the water pail didn't have enough left in it to prime.

I don't expect to live through the supper hour, especially when Aunt Hobby sits down beside me.

"We're best friends, so there!" Aunt Hobby says, throwing an arm around me. "I'm sorry I locked you down in that dark cellar."

I stare at her. She's grinning. Her arm is a cold damp tombstone on my bare neck. I try to lift it off. She keeps it fastened tight until Grandma fills her plate and tells her that under no circumstances is she to try and eat with her left hand. I can still feel the weight of her arm through dessert, which is tapioca pudding. Fish eyes and glue, my brother and I call it. I hate it. Aunt Hobby gobbles hers up and I give her mine.

I'm Aunt Hobby's best friend. She keeps saying that. She throws her arm around my neck after supper and holds me in a headlock while she shows me every piece of her handiwork.

Grandma has to tell her to leave me alone, that best friends don't pester each other all the time.

The next day is cool and rainy. It would be a relief if Aunt Hobby wasn't so restless. She's out of wool in the horrible purples and browns and maroons she likes. Embroidering doesn't interest her. Grandma's offer to draw the pattern for another rag rug she can work on makes Aunt Hobby so angry she throws her rug hook like a spear. It just misses Grandma. Then she picks up a darning needle and starts sticking it into the scabs on her left wrist. Grandma says that's enough and takes all her handiwork tools away from her until she can behave. She says her eyes are too tired anyway. I figure they're too tired from spending so many sunny hours in the cellar, but I don't say so. If it wasn't spitting rain again, I'd go out to our fort so I wouldn't have to listen to Aunt Hobby complaining.

She heaves herself out of her chair and starts stomping around the veranda, yelling that she's the only one in the whole wide world without something to do.

"Why don't you go sit in the car and pretend you're driving by the pool hall on Main Street?" my brother says.

"Shut your trap!" she shouts, and stamps her foot down on two of his tin soldiers, squashing them.

"I know just the thing to keep you busy," Grandma says.

We all hold our breath.

"You can make those beautiful wax paper windows we've read about in the *Girl's Own Annual*."

Aunt Hobby stops pacing.

"Out you go for some pretty leaves and weeds. Put on your rain coat. I'll build up a good fire in the cookstove and put on the sadirons."

We all enjoy about twenty minutes of peace and quiet.

"Watch me! Watch me!" Aunt Hobby calls from the kitchen side of the veranda. "Come and watch. You'll learn how to make wax paper windows."

I'm reading *Dorothy Dix Wins Her Wings*, lying on my camp cot under the Sunbonnet Girl quilt Aunt Hobby made. I'm on the second last chapter, "What Happened in the Wine Cellar".

"Come and watch," Aunt Hobby yells again.

"I'm too busy," I answer. The villains are calling Dorothy "Miss Wildcat", and they're planning to murder her.

Mother and Grandma are practising bridge hands, and my brother has moved his war of the tin soldiers underneath their card table.

"I'm going to make one right now," Aunt Hobby yells. "Come and watch me."

Mother and Grandma sigh.

"Why don't you just go for a minute and admire what she's doing?" Mother says to me. "That's all she wants."

"Why not him?" I ask.

"Boys don't iron stuff," my brother says. "Anyways, you're her best friend, not me."

"Come on, pal. I'll let you make one all by yourself after I teach you how," Aunt Hobby calls.

I close my book, kick off the quilt, and go around the veranda to the kitchen.

She has a piece of wax paper on the ironing board. Her specimens are laid out on it: a mustard-coloured butterfly, two dandelion leaves and a thistle bloom on its stem.

I watch as she moves them around very slowly until she's satisfied with their arrangement. She puts another piece of wax paper over them, goes to the cookstove, snaps a wooden handle on a sadiron, licks her finger and touches it to the plate to make sure it's hot enough to sizzle her spit, and then she presses the sadiron down in the centre of her picture. She lifts the iron up, presses it down again in another place, and runs it back and forth from top to bottom and from side to side.

"There!" she says, standing back. "How do you like it?"

The butterfly and thistle head have burst all around themselves. Green shadows bleed away from the thistle stem and from the teeth of the dandelion leaves. A strong smell like rancid fat and freshly cut grass makes me feel like gagging.

"Now watch."

She takes her creation off the ironing board, carries it into the room in the centre of the veranda where there's a glass window, dabs some glue in the corners of a pane, and gently presses her collage against it.

"There! See? A stained glass window just as nice as the one in the church I'll marry the Laroche twins in," she says.

It's a dull day and the window looks out onto the veranda. The light filtering through her fragile transparency isn't bright. What she has made is both ugly and beautiful. Things that were alive only minutes ago form the blurred colours and shapes of summer. The scorch marks around the edges frame them in a soft golden glow.

"There now. I need three more for the other window panes. You can do the next one. We'll take turns."

She puts another piece of wax paper on the ironing board, lays two dandelion heads on it, and shakes a moth out of a jar. It lands beside them.

"Quick! Get the hot iron," she says.

The moth is alive and she's holding it down with her thumb while she reaches for the other sheet of wax paper.

I hit her hand. The moth flutters to the floor.

"This is stupid," I cry. "Stupid and cruel. I hate it. Don't call me your best friend ever again."

Swift as a wizard she snaps a handle onto the hot sadiron, lifts it from the stove, and turns to face me.

I scream and step back.

She slaps the hot iron against her cheek, against the hairy mole. "Stupid!" she shouts. "Ugly creature! I hate you!"

Mother and Grandma and my brother come running into the kitchen, screaming and shouting. I'm standing there, stunned, holding my hands against my own burning cheeks, horrified at what Aunt Hobby has done.

Aunt Hobby is going for the long car ride she wanted, but she isn't excited. Grandma says she doesn't have any choice, she has to give in, follow the doctor's orders and do what's best to protect Hazel from herself until she gets through this stage of sudden violent outbursts.

The white salve on Aunt Hobby's face makes her look like a ghost. She refuses to roll down her window when Grandma asks her to and she's staring at me through the smudged glass.

"Why's she looking at me?" I ask.

Mother squeezes my hand and whispers, "I don't know. Maybe she's seeing herself. The way she used to look before those dreadful illnesses. Try and smile at her."

I hate to think I remind anyone of Aunt Hobby at any stage in her life. But she's leaving. I do my best to smile.

Aunt Hobby has made the hundred-mile return portion of her long car ride in the back of the district's new ambulance-hearse. I can't help thinking how much she would have loved to ride up front in it, beside the uniformed driver, and go both ways up and down Main Street past the pool hall, lights blinking, siren whining. But, after almost thirty years in Weyburn, first in the institution, then in an approved boarding house, she has been brought back to her home town to be buried beside Grandma.

There are only three of us at her graveside. Mother squeezes my elbow. "Do you remember the last holiday Hazel spent with us at the lake?" she asks while we wait for the elderly minister to find the right place in The Order For The Burial Of The Dead.

I nod my head.

"You were very kind to her," Mother says. "I was proud of you."

I remember standing on the cellar door and the sound of Aunt Hobby's shoes thudding on the rungs of the ladder, her frightened, angry grunts.

"Our dear sister and aunt," the minister says in his quavery voice, "cut down like a flower, here departed . . . "

Sudden Squalls

One of those tricks the weather can play turned Labour Day 1943 into what felt like a record breaking scorcher. The sky was blue flame and the sun squeezed chokecherry stones out of shriveled skins, making that bitter wine scent in the air. There wasn't a breath of breeze.

My parents were trying to get organized to take the things that weren't mouse and moisture proof up to Indian Head for winter storage in Gran's attic. I was sitting under the double ash tree waiting for them to leave. *War And Peace* was open on my lap, but I wasn't reading it. I was thinking about its title and the promise that World War II was ending.

My father said the Axis was finally being blasted apart and the Allies would win the war before we came back to the lake to open the cottage again. There were ads in my mother's magazines for electric stoves and refrigerators that began with: AFTER THE WAR ENJOY A NEW . . . and, TOMORROW'S PEACE WILL BRING THE PLEASURE OF A MODERN . . . I was going to start high school and the opening of Central Collegiate had been delayed until after the Victory Harvest.

But promises of victory and peace didn't mean summers would be like they used to be down at our end of Lake Katepwa, not the way the war was turning out for the Laroche twins.

First Joe Laroche was sent back from overseas with shell shock and put in some hospital in Ontario. He got out of there and hitchhiked home to Lily and the kids at No Man's Land, but he wasn't the same person without his twin brother Jimmy. We'd only seen him at night from a distance, either by himself in the boat just drifting on the black water, or alone in the truck driving by to roam the valley for junk he'd started collecting that summer. Everyone said Joe would be his old friendly self again once Jimmy got home from the war. And then, at the end of July, Jimmy Laroche was listed as Missing In Action in the invasion of Sicily.

Before the war, the Laroche twins and their grandfather, Mr. Martell, almost lived at our place. They were always coming over to show my father how to fix things up and we never opened or closed the cottage without their help.

"Hey!" my brother yelled. "What's old Sad Sack waiting for? Christmas?" He had one bare foot on the running board of the car and his index finger aimed at me.

"Never mind her. Hop in and batten the hatches," Dad yelled back at him. "It's hotter than Hades! Let's get moving!"

"How come she gets to sit in the shade pretending to read that tome she's been lugging round all summer?" Bruce asked.

Mother was in the front seat with a stack of wool blankets beside her. She was looking forward to a nice frosty glass of Canada Dry the second they got to Gran's. That was all she talked about while we hauled stuff up to the car. "Your sister would be carsick before we got up to the road in this oven," Mother said. "Do you want her sitting beside you? Be a soldier about it, Son."

Bruce fired some shots at me with his finger and dove into the trench he'd made in the bedding that filled the back seat.

"Look after things until we get back," Dad called, "and, for God's sake, cheer up. By this time next year you'll be fighting with your brother to ride in the truck with the Laroche twins, want to bet? Jimmy'll be back, you'll see." He tooted the horn.

Mattresses were tied on the car roof with binder twine. The trunk gaped open around the mouse-torn bottom of Gran's needlepoint rocker. As the Chev's underbelly scraped along the ridge of the trail, dandelions were beheaded and clumps of grass torn up. Explosions of oily exhaust shot toward me. The car lurched through the ditch, crunched onto the gravel road, the engine coughed — and backfired!

I didn't flinch. I was ironed to the tree trunk by the sun. My muscles and nerves had melted.

The horn was a dying siren.

Peace. Finally, peace.

A chokecherry stone landed on *War And Peace* with a plip. Bits of purple-black skin were still stuck to it. I flicked the stone off and rubbed at the stain. As if it mattered. The book belonged to Gran and she'd scribbled on every page of it. She'd gone down the cast of characters in the Reader's Guide Bookmark and changed all the Russian names: Kurágin to Kerr, Bezúkhov to Best, Bolkónski to Baker, and Natásha to just plain Nora. Then, as she read, Gran had used her thick-nibbed fountain pen to stroke out Tolstoy's names and write her own in above them. I found it confusing. I kept trying to figure out what the original names were and it slowed down my reading. That's why I'd had the book all summer and had only gotten as far as, "A Name Day At The Ross's" — or Rostovs' — in Book One. The war with Napoleon hadn't even started yet.

I thought about what it was like when Great Britain declared war on Hitler. It was the day before Labour Day. The twins and Mr. Martell were helping Dad take out the dock. Gran made a special trip out to the lake to tell us the news. Everyone seemed so pleased and excited. The men clapped each other on the back, shook hands, and stopped for a beer to celebrate. The twins said they were going to enlist in the army right after harvest and fight in the same tank crew. My father said he was going into the navy, that he'd been too young for the first World War, but he sure as hell wasn't too old for this one. The way they were talking made it sound as if the war wasn't going to hurt anyone we knew. It was as if the war was going to be fought by Mackenzie King and Hitler at the Regina fairgrounds and we could all go and sit in the grandstands to watch Mr. King win, the way the war happened in the dream I had about it that night.

I dreamt Miss McVeety took our Grade 5 class to the war. We had to line up behind her in pairs, the short ones like me and Squirt Samson at the front, just like Miss Weir made us do when she took our Grade 4 class to Albert Street Bridge to see the King and Queen ride by in their carriage. I didn't like walking beside Squirt Samson. He always wet his pants during arithmetic or whenever we did anything exciting. But I didn't want to miss World War II. We had little Union Jack flags on sticks to carry like the ones they gave us for the Royal Visit. When we got to the fairgrounds, bands were playing, cannons were firing, and our soldiers and sailors and airmen were marching around the field with rifles on their shoulders that had red maple leaves sticking out of the muzzles. I waved at the Laroche twins, although I knew they couldn't wave back during a war. They looked so handsome and brave in their uniforms. I didn't see my father. Mr. Churchill turned out to be the referee. His cigar was a whistle that sounded a lot like one on a train, but louder. After Mr. King blasted Hitler into bits of confetti, Mr. Churchill blew his whistle so hard I got an earache. We all jumped up on the benches, waved our flags wildly, and cheered at the top of our lungs. When I tried to sing "O Canada" and "God Save The King" after we'd won the war, my throat felt all raw and splotchy and I'd lost my voice.

I woke up the next morning with German measles. Somebody came and put a quarantine sign on our front door when we got back to Regina. I had to stay in bed with the window blinds pulled down tight and I wasn't allowed to read. My father moved the big console radio into my bedroom from the living room so I could listen to "The Happy Gang" and "Ma Perkins". He came and sat on the foot of my bed to listen to the BBC News on shortwave. Hearing the announcer's deep voice with its British accent fade in and out of my darkened room was like listening to God, I thought, Gran always claimed God was an Englishman. It was comforting to know He was on our side, but it was scary to hear God talking about storm troopers and panzer divisions and the Luftwaffe dropping bombs on innocent people. Hitler wasn't dead. The war was just starting.

Jimmy and Joe didn't wait until after harvest to enlist. They stopped at Gran's to say good-bye and she drove them into Regina so they wouldn't have to hitchhike. The twins stayed at our house the night before they joined up. We talked about how they'd always done important things as a team: marrying Lily and Faye in a double ceremony, making bricks from the clay cliff to build their cabins, going harvesting and hunting and fishing. Now, they were going to hunt the Hun together in a tank. My father said it was only natural for them to stick together, they were from the same seed. But it was because they were identical twins that the army decided to separate them. The recruiting officer thought it would drive any sergeant nuts trying to tell them apart. So my father wrote Joe, the oldest by two minutes, and explained to him how to use a special army regulation for brothers to *claim* Jimmy into the 1st Division with him.

My father seemed to know everything about fighting the war on land, in the air, on the sea and, especially, under it. At the dinner table he told us about the Green Hornet submarine he commanded that searched out and destroyed Nazi wolf packs to protect Allied convoys. Most of his stories sounded as true as an "Eyes And Ears Of The World" newsreel at the movies.

Bruce collected the little silver submarines that came in the oatmeal cereal, fueled them by putting baking soda in their tails, and pretended they were performing the same daring exploits Dad had described. He played war with those submarines in the lake, in our wash basins, and in the dishpan. Once, he even sent them to battle in my turtle bowl, almost scaring the poor creatures to death. Gran had given me George and Elizabeth for my thirteenth birthday and they hardly ever poked their heads out of their shells after that incident.

Dad's stories always reminded me of a Rogers Majestic ad that had an illustration of a submarine commander at his periscope and a man in a hard hat above him, watching him with both envy and pride. Over the factory worker's head it said: IN SPIRIT HE TOO SERVES UNDER THE SEAS.

In fact, my father was only a surgeon-lieutenant in the Queen City Sea Cadets. He did have a gold-braided uniform and I could tell he loved wearing it by the way he strutted through the house in it. But his Green Hornet submarine was just the HMCS Queen, a *ship* that was landlocked in part of the Regina Winter Club on the north bank of Wascana Creek. I went there to figure skate and play badminton. My father went there twice a week to give medicals to boys about my age who couldn't wait to grow old enough to go to war. They never thought about getting shell-shocked or going missing in action during an invasion.

War! And peace. Peace without any promises.

It wasn't shady under the ash tree anymore. Only charred looking branches with a few leaves that were sizzled and curled lay on the hot hearth of sky above me. A fire-bombed boulevard pictured in *Life* magazine had trees along it that looked leafier. The ash are the last trees in the valley to get their leaves in the spring and the first to lose them in the fall. But they're the Qu'Appelle's tall trees. They've been growing in the valley since the fourth great glacier melted, according to Mr. Martell, and he said ash trees have many stories to tell if we only knew how to listen.

I was more interested in listening to true stories than to legends. Learning how to make accurate observations and get the facts right were what was important to me. I planned to be a famous foreign correspondent, complete with dirty trench coat, a Veronica Lake hairstyle, and Katharine Hepburn's sophistication. I'd find Jimmy in Sicily and the sight of me would cure his amnesia. Then I'd cover the war-torn capitals of Europe surrounded by colleagues and lovers who looked like Ernest Hemingway, Humphrey Bogart and Alan Ladd. After my reports were filed, I would join them at a secluded sidewalk cafe to sip goblets of wine and they would toast my success. I saw myself flourish a mauve French cigarette in a long ivory holder — making scribbles of smoke over their handsome moonlit faces — as I emphasized the insignificance of all the Pulitzer Prizes I'd won since my first one for the war and peace story about the Laroche twins.

But it was sweat and not my Veronica Lake hairdo I brushed off my face. It wasn't in my plans to be burnt to a crisp under my favourite ash tree with a monument like *War And Peace* on my lap, not on the last day of my thirteenth summer at Katepwa, the last summer of the war. I wanted to circle our end of the lake to say my farewells. And, if I could drum up the courage, maybe stop to say so long to Lily and Joe and the Laroche kids.

The dirt steps to the shore were warm flannelette under my bare feet. It was as hot as July and it didn't look right to see the dock piled up on the bank. We were always either having winter or getting ready for it, I thought. I tried to remember what it was like to feel freezing cold, to have icicles instead of sweat dripping off my nose. Suddenly I realized the lake wasn't pea soup with algae any more, the way it had been for weeks, like it always was from mid-August until we left, the way it stayed until freeze-up, Mr. Martell said. It was magic! The water was crystal clear and as smooth as a magnifying glass. I picked up a flat stone from the bottom and skipped it. It made four circles and sank. The war had lasted four long summers and its last summer had been the worst one. Jimmy missing, Joe sick. This damned war. All we used to worry about was our war with the weather. Violence and destruction only meant our dock had been washed away again in a storm.

I'm watching them put our dock up for the third time and it's only the first week of July.

"Sure can't trust the weather this year," Daddy says.

"No time," Mr. Martell says. "Lake got named Sudden Squalls Water on account of how fast them bad storms come up out of nowheres."

"Makes good steady work fixing Doc's dock," Joe says, and grins at me. "Doc's dock," he says again. "Sounds funny, eh?"

Daddy takes one of the broken boards the twins and I found down by the dam and floats it over to Mr. Martell. "Funny how things down here got named," he says.

"Yeah!" Jimmy shoots a spray of water at me with his hand. "Like me an Joe naming Miss Lazybones the Super for always hanging round watching us work."

"Like that," Daddy says, and laughs. "Though it's not quite what I was thinking. Last winter a patient lent me a missionary's journal about exploring the Qu'Appelle Valley. The legend's in it about the young brave who keeps hearing his sweetheart call his name as he paddles down our lake, then, when he gets home, he learns she died calling for him. Indians told the missionary they often heard spirits call to them from our shorelines and they would call back, 'Katapaywie?' — 'Who's calling?', so that's what they named our lake. Funny thing is, translated from French and Cree, here we are, putting this damn dock up again in Who Calls Valley in Who Calls Lake!"

"Pah!" Mr. Martell spits a nail from his mouth into his hand. He hammers it into the dock. "Priests! Ought to listen closer to what's told them. Since when's a question a name? First people named her Sudden Squalls Water soon as the big ice went out."

I skipped another stone. The circles it made linked as they got smaller and smaller, until there was nothing out there to ripple the lake's smooth skin, not even a hole where the stone sank. If there was such a thing as a perfect skipping stone, if I found it that day, if it fit my hand and I launched it with skill, it would go on and on and on — across the lake to the far shore. I began wading toward the dam, searching the bottom for it.

It's always too mucky to find anything on the bottom at the foot of the clay cliffs. I looked up. Only a few swallow holes pock-marked the steep slope. The Laroche twins had scaled that greasy clay during a cloudburst to rescue Bruce and me from the secret cave we were digging when the storm hit. Thunder was quaking the valley. The cave's mouth trembled around us like caramel pudding. I thought we were going to be buried alive.

The twins managed to tip their heavy wood rowboat up on its bow against the cliff with its flat stern under us to use as a platform. One of the twins had to stand on the other's shoulders to reach us. We couldn't tell which twin was which because their faces were smeared with clay. As we slid down the slippery cliff with the twin who pulled us from the cave's mouth, I heard the smack as it closed above us. Then, before we jumped off the boat, a crackling flash of double-forked lightning struck the lake and white-bellied fish spouted up in the geyser, spinning around in their final jumps.

What if the twins hadn't been out fishing together when the storm struck, I wondered. One of the twins couldn't have rescued us alone. I wondered what would have happened if Joe and Jimmy had been together in the invasion of Sicily. I didn't think even cliffs of burning white mud, like the cliffs of Sicily, would have defeated them if they'd been fighting together.

My father had clipped a war correspondent's report on the invasion of Sicily out of the newspaper. He pinned it to the Frosst Pharmaceuticals calendar on the cottage wall beside his war map. An unnamed soldier was quoted in it.

The soldier said that, when the davit hooks were slipped and their craft headed out for Sicily, he felt the same sort of tightness as before a squall struck back home. He was the only one of the thirty-five men on board who didn't get seasick. His buddy had thrown his guts up. Rough water was nothing new to him, he said, but then they hit the steep beach and they hit the white mud — limestone mud! The stuff stuck and burned on you worse than hot whitewash, he told the correspondent, but he was going back down in that bloody white mud to search for his buddy before their unit moved on.

Gran had circled the soldier's story with the same pen she'd used in *War And Peace* and written "Jimmy!" on it. That's what I thought too. But lime was what we put down our backhouse hole once a week.

We'd been warned never to let it touch our skin if we didn't want the flesh burned from our bones. A pinch of lime in our eyes would blind us forever, Gran often told us. I was afraid to ask if limestone mud was worse than the dry powder we used. I was afraid to think about Jimmy going back down those foreign cliffs.

Beyond the clay cliffs the bottom gets too sandy to find many good skipping stones. Most of the stones I picked up turned out to be too round, as useless to skip as skulls.

It was thick with weeds along the curve of No Man's Land, the spongy mossy kind that are full of dead crayfish. I walked over them as fast as I could, looking ahead instead of down.

The timbers of the dam were bone dry. I stepped carefully across slivers the size of silver-grey bayonets to the foot of the zigzag fish sluice. Mr. Martell's only son and his namesake, Jakey, had disappeared underneath there many years ago.

Jakey was my mother's first summertime "beau". He was thirteen years old and he swam like a fish, Gran said; she knew because she taught him how. She said he was diving for something under the dam and must have been trapped somehow at the back. His body was never found. They even tried floating a loaf of fresh bread with quicksilver in the middle of it along the edge of the dam in a fish net, which was supposed to draw a drowned body up to the surface. Although it had happened a long time ago, Mr. Martell still went down to the dam a lot and sat on the bottom bin of the fish sluice, staring into the sluggish river.

I crouched down beside the sluice and leaned over the edge of the dam to see what it looked like under the place Jakey had disappeared. Something glinted near the front of the cavern where the murky light met the darkness. It looked like a stone with gold flecks on it. Was that what Jakey had been diving for, I wondered. Its underside would be crawling with bloodsuckers. Did I have the nerve to get it? Jakey would have scraped the bloodsuckers off on the rough boards of the dam, carried the stone in his hand, polishing it smoother and smoother, waiting for a day just like Labour Day 1943 when he didn't have to watch for the waves to unfold a good path. Jakey would have climbed up to the lip of the dam, adjusted the stone in his hand, leaned into his throw, and called out the count as the perfect skipping stone made a chain of circles joining the shorelines.

"Super! Hey, Super!" somebody called.

I turned my head quickly. Just for a split second I thought I saw the Laroche twins leaning against the only ash tree on the tip of No Man's Land. The tree, and the willows and bulrushes in front of it, were splashed with dazzling sun patches.

"Don't youse dare dive into there!" the voice called. "Quicksand under them boards'd suck youse to China."

"Who's there?" I called. "Joe? Is that you?" I looked down at the water again. The stone had disappeared. I shielded my eyes and scanned the shoreline. I couldn't see a soul anywhere.

Joe's circle of salvage around the Laroche cabins hadn't grown much wider since word came from the War Office about Jimmy. A part coyote mutt scrambled out of a truck fender and ambled over to me for a sniff, then flopped down in the warm sand at my feet. Another dog lifted its head from a shady bed in the rubble and howled at the sun. It was strange to hear that lonesome nighttime sound in broad daylight, a warning, as if the dog had sensed how Joe felt about the sun since he'd gotten home.

Fear of the sun was part of Joe's shell shock right from the beginning. After they got the news about Jimmy, Joe began acting as if he was afraid of the moon, too, Lily told Mother and Gran one afternoon while they were having tea. He would only leave the cabin on the blackest nights, she said, and she didn't know what to do about it. Mother just shook her head and patted Lily's arm. Gran took her false teeth out of the tea slops and put them back in her mouth, got *The Book of Common Prayer* out of her knitting bag, opened it at the bookmark ribbon, sucked her teeth for a minute, and said, "This is my favourite psalm, Lily:

> "I will lift up mine eyes
> unto the hills
> from whence cometh my help.
> The Lord himself is my keeper.
> He will see that the sun shall
> not burn me by day:
> neither the moon by night."

She took her fountain pen out of her blouse pocket and circled what she'd just read. "There now," she said. "Tell Joseph I'm not trying to convert him to High Anglican, but, if he'll read this, he'll see he isn't the first one to need help coping with God's elements." Then she slipped the book's leather carrying strap over Lily's wrist.

So I knew Joe wasn't crazy when I overheard the two men talking about him in the cafe at the main beach. Gran probably would have used her cane on them.

"You heard about that nut case lives down by the dam?" the guy with the oily hair asked. "Got a loaded Luger and live hand grenades inside a kind of war zone round his place on No Man's Land."

"You mean Loony Laroche," the other one said, tapping his pimply forehead and smirking.

"That's him. Crazy bugger's AWOL from some army loony bin down east, I heard. He's one of them squatters lives in the whitewashed cabins down there. Got a herd of kids all sorts of colours from brown to black. Lives with that nigger gal. Bastard's got an arsenal could blow the dam to kingdom come."

They were slumped over a table in a booth, sucking on yellow cigarette stubs, and scratching at their crotches and hairy armpits. I went over and rapped on the table top with the stick of the Torpedo sucker I'd just bought. "Did I hear you say you're friends of Joe Laroche's?" I asked. "Army buddies of his?"

If looks could kill, I would've dropped dead.

"Oh, pardon me," I said loudly, "I can see you're not buddies of a war hero like Joseph Laroche. You're just a couple of zombies, aren't you?" My legs were shaking so badly I thought I was going to crumple into a heap at their feet. Only the feeling that I'd done something braver than they ever would gave me the strength to turn and walk slowly away from them.

But there I was that Labour Day, standing like a zombie in front of what some jerk had called Joe's war zone. What did I have to fear? I knew Joe hadn't planted any land mines in there.

The Laroche kids played war games in and over and around the parts of wrecked vehicles all the time. The boys used tin cans filled with sand for their grenades. A rusted farm tractor without its engine or treads was their tank. They crowded into the windowless, doorless, truck cab to fly their bombing missions, during which each of the crew members was responsible for his own sound effects: the pilot for his whining, coughing engine; the tailgunners for the staccato splutters of their machine guns; the bombardiers for enhancing the explosions of their hubcap-bombs as they landed square on their targets. The Laroche girls ran a Red Cross hospital in the half-crushed compartment of a panel truck that had once belonged to a florist. You could still make out the slogan in faded red paint on its side: SAY IT WITH FLOWERS, SAY IT WITH OURS. The nurses pretended to boil water in old pots and pans on a broken coal oil stove and, if none of the boys would co-operate and get wounded, they dragged one of the reluctant, but patient, dogs into their hospital to bandage.

Where were the kids? They would have told me if it was okay to go in and thank Joe for warning me about the quicksand. They knew me. I'd ridden in the back of the truck with them to the main beach, up to Gran's house in Indian Head, and when they went around the lake to sell vegetables to the summer people. We were practically family

— except they got to live year round at the lake and I didn't. We had Lily in common. Lily had mothered me, too. They knew she'd been my nursemaid when I was a child, that she'd comforted me during bad storms too by telling me thunder was only God rolling watermelons under his bed. They'd heard the stories about how my parents brought Lily up with us from Alabama that summer and introduced her to the twins, how she'd fallen in love with everything about the valley, had discovered that her legends and Mr. Martell's were often the same, and how she'd finally gotten my mother's wedding dress to wear when she married Joe. Lily always said it didn't matter to her which "lil boogers" were hers by birth or the sweet Lord's arrangements. We're all of us God's children, Lily told us, white or coloured, good and bad. She said that even Jimmy's wife Faye was one of the good Lord's family — loved by Him equally as the rest of us, in spite of her running off on her children after the twins joined up.

Gran said Faye used to smack the kids around, drink like a fish, steal things like a magpie, and, no use pretending otherwise, was a loose woman. Faye was a born camp follower, Gran said, and only the dear Lord knew where she'd end up, or how many other innocent babies she'd bring into the world and abandon. Mother always reminded Gran that Faye had done at least one good deed for Jimmy's youngsters by leaving them behind to be jumbled together under Lily's wing — let's give Faye credit for that much, anyway, Mother would say.

So what was I afraid of? Faye wasn't going to rush out and slap my face. Lily went in and out of that circle of scrap as if it wasn't there. She acted as if the yard was as neat as a pin, like it had been before the war, and the way she and the kids had kept it until Joe came home with shell shock. The war zone hadn't stopped her from going out to clean cabins at Sunset Inn or delivering the sweet smelling laundry she did for us at Mr. Martell's. She still took truckloads of kids to Mass at Lebret on Sunday mornings, off to swim at the main beach when it was green at our end of the lake, on picnics and berry picking. Lily hadn't lost her peacetime smile and good humour. Joe wasn't violent, his strange behaviour didn't frighten her, it just worried her how much sicker he'd gotten after Jimmy went missing in Sicily and she couldn't do anything about it except pray.

Really, I thought, what did I have to fear?

My father said Joe hadn't meant to build a barrier against neighbours and friends with the ring of junk he'd collected. And Joe knew me. Sure, I'd grown up a lot since he and Jimmy went away to war, but hadn't he just called me by their old nickname down at the dam? I didn't think it would be a good idea to just barge in and surprise Joe, though.

It was positively eerie to stand there rubbing the mutt's flank with my bare foot and not a single Laroche to be seen or heard. I just couldn't get up the nerve to pick my way through the junk and knock on the cabin door. I gave up.

The mutt followed me past Mr. Martell's Victory Garden, where I mentally moved the H in his RUHBARB FOR SALE sign on the gate, and into the churchyard, where he stretched out in the shade of the tall tombstone with the scary inscription:

> Stranger,
> pause as you go by.
> As you are now,
> so once was I.
> As I am now,
> soon you will be.
> Prepare in life
> to follow me.

War! The dates were 1900-1918. That was the war my father said was supposed to end all wars. I wished for the power to make all wars, past and present, like my dream of World War II. I wished for the power to skip that tombstone across the lake as if it was the magic skipping stone. I looked up at the hills.

When Mr. Martell won stone-skipping competitions with my father, which was every time they had one, he always said it was because he'd found a petrified slice of ice-rock from the glacier up on the hills. My father never said that was impossible.

Half-way up Daddy Long Legs Hill I had to sit down and rest. The heat was blistering. It was a crazy quest anyway, I thought. I didn't believe in magic or legends or fairy tales, only in facts.

The valley was all hard glossy colours, like a *National Geographic* cover of a magic sunken garden. It looked as if a necklace of precious metals and stones had been dropped around the Laroche cabins. Across the lake, there was just an ink line of clouds along the top of the hills that held the flat wheat fields up to the sun.

I heard the Chev's horn blasting, saw it come scooting around the bend in the road by No Man's Land, raising a tunnel of dust behind it. It was bouncing along like a jackrabbit.

I ran down to meet them at the top of the trail. Dad slowed down and I hopped on the running board.

Bruce had his head hanging out the back window like a dog's, and he was panting. "Gran sent you a soggy cucumber sandwich," he said, pretending to gag. "I didn't mean to sit on it." He was hoping I wouldn't notice he had his door partly open so he could leap out before the car stopped and beat me into the cottage.

I wasn't in the mood for childish games. We were closing the cottage, not opening it. When he threw his door open and ran, I stepped off the running board and went back and sat down under the double ash tree. I opened *War And Peace* where I'd left Gran's messy bookmark: "Dear Countess, what an age," I read.

"What's all this?" Bruce yelled from inside the veranda. "There's a whole bunch of junk in here that doesn't belong to us."

"Don't be silly," Mother said.

"No kidding!" Bruce yelled. "Looks like old Sad Sack must've been robbing Loony Laroche's junk heap."

I put *War And Peace* down and stood up.

"Hush, Bruce," Mother said. "You know how voices carry at the lake on a still day. Don't be rude about poor Joe."

"How many times do I have to tell you Joe Laroche is a war hero?" Dad yelled, marching into the veranda behind mother. "Don't ever let me hear you speak of him that way again! Not ever!"

"Oh!" Mother exclaimed. "Good heavens! Look!"

I went over to look through the veranda screen.

"What the hell's this?" Dad picked up a round stone with a handle on it. "My old knife sharpener? I haven't laid eyes on this damn thing since meat rationing — maybe before." He rolled the stone around with his thumb.

"The Quints!" Mother cried. She showed my father a framed colour photograph of the Dionne babies, lying on their stomachs all in a row, looking at him looking at them. "You know, I always thought they were the spitting image of Jimmy and Faye's little ones. Didn't you? Where on earth did this come from after so many years?"

Maybe Faye needed it, I thought. Maybe she had to be reminded that she could love her babies a lot if they were clean and quiet and well dressed and smiling like that.

"Hey! The missing subs from my fleet!" Bruce held up the Blue Willow chamber pot I'd been accused of chucking into the bushes several summers before. I could hear some of his silly submarines skittering around in it.

"The foot of the old brass bed," Mother squealed. "Hurray! We won't have to prop the foot on the black bedding box any more. How many years has this been missing? Ten? Fifteen? More?"

"You know, I never did have time to use these damn things," Dad said in a low voice. "Bought 'em and forgot 'em." He had a set of wood carving tools in his hands. Long delicate looking chisels gleamed on a bed of maroon velvet in an oak box.

There was a quilt Gran had won first prize for at the Regina Fair; a rug Aunt Hobby had hooked with HOME SWEET HOME on it; and some wild coloured afghans that Gran had crocheted from scraps.

It was like Christmas in there.

"Tra-lah, tra-lah," Mother sang, doing a sort of graceful majorette routine with a pair of Indian Clubs she said she hadn't seen since she was a girl.

"And look here," Dad said. He handed Mother a blue leather book with gold lettering on its cover.

"Our old Sudden Squalls Haven Guest Book," Mother said. "My parents used this when they first built this cottage." She read out some names and some comments about the magical quality of the Qu'Appelle Valley. Then she stopped near the back of the book. "Oh!" she said. "Oh, Lord!" She touched one hand to her lips, just the fingertips, and then touched them to the page. "See you next summer," she whispered. "Yours truly, Jakey Martell."

My father put his arm around her and she leaned against his sweat-stained shirt.

There was a distant growl of thunder. I stepped back and looked up at the sky. Thunderheads like ragged coal piles were spilling toward our side of the lake. Their edges were lit by licks of the fire-red sun.

Dad gave orders. We worked quickly in spite of the steamy hotness. Some of the things were carried into the closed-in room in the centre of the cottage to be stored for the winter. The afghans, the quilt, rug, sharpening stone and wood carving tools were carried up to the car and packed in the back seat so they would be handy to give back to the Laroches.

But my father was worried. "Why would Joe return these things now? He's had them for years. What's going through his head?" Dad said. "We'll have to stop long enough for me to have a talk with him. Maybe I can convince him Jimmy's going to be home soon. Joe's a proud man. You've all got to back me up when I tell him the children were playing on our veranda and left these things behind."

Bruce delayed our leaving. He wanted to finish printing instructions for how to fuel his submarines and draw diagrams of the Green Hornet's battles for the Laroche boys to follow. Neither of our parents got testy about the delay and told Bruce to get a wiggle on. They were proud of him for sharing, they said.

I went up to wait in the car. I had *War And Peace* on my lap, closed tight. It sounded as if the entire Luftwaffe was roaring our way above the churning black clouds. If the trail got too wet, we wouldn't make it up to the highway.

It was as dark as midnight when we pulled in at Mr. Martell's to leave him the keys for the padlocks. Huge drops of rain made separate circles in the dust on the windshield. We cranked up our windows. Suddenly the wind slammed against the car, rocking it from side to side.

"Out!" Dad yelled. "Grab hands! Let's go! Follow me!"

The wind was hotter than a blast from a furnace. It was hard to breathe. The rain drops were bullets. Dirt and leaves and tree branches hit us like shrapnel.

Mr. Martell pulled us inside just as the storm hit full force. Dad and Mr. Martell grabbed the chesterfield cushions and held them against the window panes. Mother and Bruce and I crouched behind the chesterfield, arms over our heads, expecting the roof to be torn off, the house to explode. The ceiling was a sieve. Water poured down on the linoleum, rushed under the door in a muddy river. We are in a submarine at the bottom of the ocean, I thought, it's going to burst apart any second and we'll be swept away in the debris. Then the deafening noise stopped.

The wind dropped as suddenly as it had come up. Thunder rolled off down the valley. Candle-like lightning lit the room briefly and snuffed itself out. I could count to fifteen before the soft groans of thunder that followed it. That was when we heard Lily screaming Joe's name, over and over, louder and louder.

The door flew open and Lily stood there, stiff and soundless, hanging onto the door frame. She could have been the scarecrow in Mr. Martell's Victory Garden. Twigs were stuck in her hair. Her sky-blue dress, the one she starched to a shine to wear visiting, was covered with mud and soaking wet, plastered to her thin body as tight as skin.

Mother ran over to her and wrapped her arms around her. "What's happened?" she said. "What is it, Lily? Tell me."

"Joe. Joe's real sick. Lord, Mizz Vee, soon's the storm made it dark he done took on ahollering for Jimmy." Lily's voice began to rise to a keen. "Soon's the dark came Joe done cut loose for the boat. Lord? Sweet Jesus? He done gone out on that black water to search for his brother." She tore herself away from Mother and disappeared into the darkness outside.

The yard was a sea of black mud, sticky, but slick as wet clay. I was down on my hands and knees. Up again, trying to lift my giant mudded feet and run. It was still hot — hotter than Hades. The air was so heavy I felt like I was swimming under water.

Slipping, sliding down the lake bank, I made it to the shore, and ran along it toward the sound of the men's voices shouting Joe's name.

Crossing the dam was crazy. The wind was back up again. It had changed directions. It would bring the storm back, worse than before, the way it often happened at Katepwa. The lake surged over the dam, a waterfall. Weeds wrapped my ankles, my calves, my knees. Double-back storms only hit in July — at the beginning of summers, not at the end of them. I would be swept down into the river, washed under the dam's edge into Jakey's tomb, sucked into the quicksand.

Half-crawling, half-swimming, I got to the fish sluice, grabbed hold of its side, scrambled over it into the top bin. I looked back at No Man's Land.

Blackness! Nothing but blackness. My eyes were chokecherry stones. "Joe? Jimmy? Where — are — you?" I cried, trying to force my eyes to see somebody, something, anything — a blacker shadow in the blackness. Was I under the dam? In the quicksand, sinking deeper?

A giant flashtube of lightning exploded in my eyes — a fireball of white light, and then pitch blackness again, tar, and I saw them. Sharp and clear as daylight, I saw them.

They were standing in front of the ash tree. I saw the mole beside Jimmy's right eye, the dimple at the left corner of Joe's mouth. They had their arms around each other's shoulders. They were smiling. The Laroche twins stood tall in their army uniforms, motionless, smiling at me.

My father and Mr. Martell were beside them, bent over the splintered bow of the boat. I cupped my mouth with my hands to yell at them to look up, the war was over and Jimmy was home, the twins were together again.

Another flash of lightning burned the twins from my eyes before I got out a sound. Only my father and Mr. Martell were there, crouched on the shore of No Man's Land. I covered my eyes.

Then I heard the twins' voices calling my name.

There are other Katepwa oldtimers who'll tell you that Joe Laroche ran off to Halifax during that storm on Labour Day 1943. They'll say that somebody's husband, or boyfriend, or cousin came home from the war in forty-five willing to swear on a stack of bibles he'd seen Joe in the Halifax harbour when his troop ship disembarked there. Joe is supposed to have said he was going to hitch a ride on the first ship to Sicily to claim his twin brother Jimmy and bring him home to the valley where he belonged.

But nobody stood a chance of getting out of the valley while the storm tore its way back and forth through it, not even Joe. The gazebo was torn off the top of Pimple Hill; lightning struck the Katepwa Hotel twice, causing a fire the second time that destroyed the screen veranda and the wicker furniture in it; the waves were so high they undercut the bank at our end of the lake and our cottage collapsed on the shore.

Joe's body was never found, not a trace of it. Neither was Jimmy's in Sicily, although he wasn't officially declared Killed In Action until after VE Day.

Lily and the children moved to a house Gran owned in Indian Head before the first blizzard hit that fall. Mr. Martell moved into town with them a year later. After that, the whitewashed cabins at No Man's Land just seemed to crumble into the sand a little bit more during each summer squall until they had disappeared too.

It seemed right to me then, back in 1943, as it still does now, that the Laroche twins aren't buried in a grave. They weren't meant to be held down by a carved stone, a stone too large to be skipped across the lake to the far shore. Visiting a monument wouldn't be the same as standing by the zigzag fish sluice, listening to their voices call my name as the waves break on the shore.

Just Another Midnight Attraction

Katepwa. At last. The familiar surroundings I need to let me concentrate on becoming a woman — a femme fatale.

Old Buffalo Back Hill on guard, green-tinged hide bristling. Mother Bunting Hill, nipple poking into the sky, and Baby Bunting tucked close to her, such an easy climb for tiger lilies to pin in my hair. And good old Daddy Long Legs with his gently sloping tentacles I raced my brother down last summer, both of us swooping and shouting that we were Batman. The things I did to break the monotony of being stuck in girlhood! Soon, I'll be strolling our hills alone, trying to decide which dreamboat I'll let take me to the midnight dance, comparing their physiques, oblivious to the guys at my feet slowing down on the highway to honk and wolf-whistle at me, the mysterious woman whose flowing black hair and fabulous figure are exactly like Hedy Lamarr's — the Hollywood star who's known to have the most beautiful body in the world. Our hills are the same, unchanged since the Ice Age, waiting to welcome me back for the summer I'll become a woman.

But our old cottage shaped like a circus tent is gone. It's only a memory, like the old flat-chested me will be if everything goes according to my plans. I guess I should look at it that way. It's just that the raw blonde structure that stands in its place has a sort of suffocating city-look about it. It hasn't got a wrap-around screen veranda to capture the breeze off the lake on hot afternoons or the first cool drafts that come down from the hills in the evenings. The frenzied excitement of sudden rainstorms is history. We won't have to rush around unhooking hundreds of big canvas shutters from the ceiling to fasten down over miles of screen. Sliding a bunch of glass windows shut won't be the same.

Tight as a drum, my father keeps saying, rapping his knuckles on the unpainted siding and tapping his fingers on putty-blotched window panes. One good thing about having windows, I discover, is that I can see myself reflected in the glass. So I'll be able to stand back from them and use them like full-length mirrors to check how my curves are developing.

Inside, the new cottage is a skeleton of two-by-four studs with knotty pine wallboards stacked on the floor. There isn't going to be any storm room in its centre, no inner sanctum, nowhere to play Monopoly and count how close the lightning is striking. The McClary range crouches where the kitchen will be some day, its flat backside displayed through the rib cage, the hole for its stove pipe gaping. It used to sit so proudly in the kitchen end of the veranda, its iron and chrome bosom thrust out for polishing with bacon fat and Bon Ami. It will probably be covered with sawdust all summer and Mother will use the smelly coal oil stove. Our old cottage was comfortable, as relaxing to hang around in as a stretched sweat shirt. I'm lucky I don't have to spend much time on public exhibit in this one while I work at becoming a woman.

My sleeping porch is twenty feet away from the new cottage. It has screen all around it, but a wide ribbon of canvas is hooked, top and bottom, over the screen on the outside. It's dark inside, but private.

The first thing I do when I get my stuff into my private retreat is review the regimen I set for myself in the diary entry I made on the last day of school:

> Use summer vacation to become a WOMAN.
> Things to do: order a New Improved Genuine Hollywood Stars' Bust Building Kit & Secret Formula Cream for Dr. P.S. Scott, c/o Lake Katepwa Post Office, Saskatchewan, Canada — (underline "in a plain brown wrapper"). Make nose splint with tongue depressors and adhesive tape from Dad's M.D. bag. Bind nose every night like picture of Japanese woman's feet in *World Progress* history text, page 207. Give up all food except lettuce and grapefruit on July 1st. Record measurements here every day, without fail. Start now: 32-26-39-2 1/4 (nose).
> PRAY FOR THE CURSE!

I mailed the order for the kit before we left Regina today. I don't have to start my diet until tomorrow.

I've got the adhesive tape and tongue depressors to use at bedtime. And, if I can figure out how to do it without the picture in my history book to look at, I don't intend to give my nose one more free night to grow as big as my father's. People are already saying, "Oh my, your daughter's the spitting image of you, Doctor," and now even sneezes give me a stomach-ache from worrying that the Cycle of Womanhood will wheel right by me without stopping.

I never need to remind myself to pray for the curse.

I pray for it while I hide my diary between the two lumpy mattresses and make my bed. I pray for it as I take off my jeans to put on my bathing suit. Then I check my underwear for the red signature of the great biological change I've been expecting for three years.

Nothing. Not even a tiny dot of blood.

I lie down on my bed and massage my head. My problem is a sluggish pituitary gland at the base of my brain. According to my father's explanations about the onset of menstruation, and from what I've read and re-read in the Kotex booklet Mother gave me when I was only eleven, that's where becoming a woman begins — in a stupid little pea-sized gland nobody can see or get at to squeeze. All it has to do is signal my ovaries to let go of just one of the hundreds of ova they've had locked in there ever since I was born. Then one tiny ovum takes a three or four day trip through my Fallopian tube to my uterus where nature will have prepared the velvety red lining of *en-doe-mee-tree-um* that I'm dying to find flowing out of my vagina. It's a gland, not God, that's to blame for me not having my first period or any breasts. I massage my head harder.

The crayfish claw I wear on a silver chain around my neck for good luck slides over into my armpit. I put it back, centre front, right where my cleavage will be when my pituitary gland and Mother Nature co-operate. I plan to buy some of those wired Gothic brassieres that boys break their fingers trying to get into. It'll be my revenge for the time that guy stuck his hands up my sweat shirt at the bonfire last summer and said, "Hey, where are they?"

I gaze up at the point where the four roof joists meet. My sleeping porch needs a ceiling. There are seven spiders up there and a possible eighth — it's either a fly, sucked dry, or a deadly black widow, a vamp who eats her own mate and is a menace to all mankind. I think it's one of those young female widows that still look just like male ones. She's hanging there, waiting to shed her baby skin, anxious to get her red hourglass beauty mark on her stomach to show she's a shiny black temptress. We're both waiting for something magic to happen to us. If she doesn't move while I blink my eyes three times and make three wishes, I decide, we'll both get what we want.

I blink. One: I wish for the curse.

I blink again. Two: I wish for breasts as voluptuous as Jane Russell's are in that publicity picture of her lying in a haystack to advertise "The Outlaw".

My last blink. Three: I wish for legs more gorgeous than Betty Grable's in her pin-up girl poster that. . . . One blink too many.

The shiny black one, a hungry black widow for sure, is bailing out of her lair in that cloud of webs up there and dropping toward me. I scream, jump off my bed, and am out the screen door in a single leap.

When I creep back into my sleeping porch with the fly swatter, there's a bumblebee, legs up, in the centre of the chenille rose in the middle of my rumpled bedspread. I swat it, flick it onto the floor, hit it again, and flip it into the corner.

It's time to put on some of my new Hubba Hubba Red lipstick and ride my bike down to the main beach. Alli is counting on me to call on her with a full report of how many dreamboats are hanging around the cafe, waiting to find someone to ask to the Dominion Day Midnight Dance tonight.

I have to stand up on the pedals most of the two miles to the main beach. There's a steady stream of traffic and I don't want anyone to see how my bum hangs over the bicycle seat.

After my bike is propped against the poplar tree stump outside the Katepwa Hotel & Cafe, I bend over and pretend to inspect the spokes. This gives me a chance to slip my hand up under my sweat shirt and down the top of my bathing suit to make sure the two washcloths are still in the right spots. Both okay. A-cups stuffed with terry towelling aren't as smooth as flesh, but they bump out my sweat shirt a bit.

Now. I've got to go in the front door of the cafe, saunter slowly down the long aisle between the booths and counter to the back door, making my inspection. The most difficult part is peering into each booth without seeming nosy. I have to examine each guy's physique first, then his face — sometimes a dreamboat can be sort of homely if he has a great muscle-man body: wide shoulders, big chest, strong looking arms. The colour of their hair and eyes is important, whether they're tall or short, and their age. Only mature older guys interest us. If they don't look at least sixteen, I don't even bother to make a snap decision about which movie star they resemble.

I straighten my shoulders, tug down the back of my bathing suit, open the cafe door, and step inside.

Katepwa's own Errol Flynn — but without the mustache — "Casanova" Danny Addison, is slouched over the linoleum table top at his regular place in the first booth. He likes to keep a close watch on who's coming and going and who plays what for whom on the jukebox. Three guys I've never seen before are sitting with him. They're not bad looking.

Van Johnson acknowledges my entrance. "Woo, woo, woo. Another jive-girl," he says, snapping his fingers and smiling at me.

Not bad. Not bad at all. I could fall for his friendly boy-next-door looks. Tyrone Power types are just too-too handsome.

"Just a young girl who shood-dunt leave her muth-er," Casanova says, and chug-a-lugs his Coke. "How's tricks, P.S.? Down for the summer?"

"Sure," I say. Now what? If I stand here long enough admiring Van Johnson's Pepsodent smile, will Casanova introduce us?

"Hey! P.S.?" Alli is down in the last booth, her chin hanging over the back of the bench like a *Kilroy Was Here* cartoon. "Ignore those wolves and come here. It's important."

So! Alli didn't wait for me to call on her with the big news about who's who in the July 1st attractions. Well, Casanova's the dreamboat she wants anyway. She won't go after Van Johnson.

As I walk down to the far end of the cafe, Casanova and his supporting cast sing along with the tune on the jukebox. "Marizy doats and doezy doats and little lambzy divey," they chorus, making me walk too fast and forget to swivel my hips.

"Bah-ah-ahd little boys bothering you?" Colleen asks as I slide into the booth beside her. Colleen? What's she doing here — in our territory? There's a sparkling coat of Hot Stuff Scarlet polish on her long fingernails — and she's smoking.

"Oh. Hi, Coll," I say. "You out for the long weekend?"

She nods, and smoke drifts out of her mouth into my face. I sneeze, and look across the table at the others. "Hi, Del — Margot." So there's five of us to celebrate the beginning of summer. And four of them. Great. "Hey, can I bum a weed?" I ask.

I know my face is still flushed pincherry red from gazing into Van Johnson's deep blue eyes. Hedy Lamarr would have just said, *Hel-low dah-ling*, and he would have followed her down here. She would have perched on the edge of the table, drawn a gold monogrammed cigarette case out of the bosom of her low-cut black lace beach coat, clicked it open, and allowed Van Johnson to take a cigarette out of it to light for her.

Alli tosses a squashed pack of Sweet Caps to me. "One left," she says, "and no matches. Get a light off Coll and let's get down to business. We're trying to decide what to do tonight — about *them*." She lowers her voice. "We just happened to, ahem, overhear their plans."

"In, dope, breathe in!" Colleen pushes her butt against the end of my bent cigarette. "Draw!" she says. "Suck in! And for gawd's sake stop your hand from shaking or I'll get the hot ash up your big nose."

"Big's better than a pimple," I say, eyeing the cute little pug nose that she thinks is too small. I take the butt out of her claws, press it against my cigarette, breathe in, and sneeze. Smoke wouldn't make Hedy sneeze. But Hedy Lamarr doesn't have a nose the size of my father's — big enough to cast a shadow on her cleavage. When I finally get my cigarette lit, I say, "Hey listen, who are those guys with Casanova? Anyone know?"

Their replies are so typical — right in character — just like their thumbnail sketches were in our high school yearbook.

Colleen snatches her butt back from me and mashes it out in the sardine tin ashtray. "A bunch of bah-ahd kids too young to be in uniform or do anything remotely exciting." (Yearbook: Hubba, hubba, hubba! — 'nough said.)

Del pats the palm of her hand up and down on the table top as if she's patting some dreamboat's brush cut hair. "They're cute as Katzenjammer Kids but beneath me," she says. "Like what guy isn't? Even Casanova's only about five-eleven." (Yearbook: Six-foot-two, eyes of blue, always smiling DOWN on you.)

"Skinny drips. Mon Dieu! Skinny dippers, I mean." Margot giggles and her enormous breasts jiggle. (Yearbook: Round and firm and fully packed, this mam-selle purrs like a real hepcat.)

I laugh. (Yearbook: She who laughs last, laughs loud, louder, loudest — and longest.)

And then there's Alli — (Yearbook: When this blonde bomber hit Central, all the dreamboats became *Alli-es!*) — she leans forward and whispers, "Those guys plan a nude swim at the main beach right at midnight. Should we, ahem, be there?"

Del sits up straight and looks over the back of my bench to see what's going on down in the first booth. "To be or not to be! That is the question!" She slumps back down.

"Thank-yew, thank-yew. Not to be. Not for me." Colleen runs her fingers back through her flaming mane of hair. "Definitely the less boring solution. There's a midnight dance, right?"

We all nod our heads.

Naked dreamboats. I don't know. Are they any different than the illustrations in my dad's medical books? And what would Van Johnson think if they caught us spying on them? I take a long drag of my cigarette and blow the smoke out of my nostrils in Colleen's face. I smile at her, flick the ash into the sardine tin, and scan the faces of Alli, Del and Margot. For them, it might be educational. Del's father has been away at the war for so many years she probably doesn't remember seeing a naked man. Margot's father is so old, his is probably all shriveled up. And Alli? She just thinks if she follows Casanova around long enough he'll finally notice her. Everyone's looking at me, waiting for my answer, except Colleen. She's examining her cuticles. "Maybe Coll wants to give our old dance intermission spy game a whirl?" I say. "The one we played when we were just kids? Did somebody tell her what we saw last July the First when we shone our flashlights in that car, and there was you-know-who practically doing it with that young war widow from Lebret?"

Alli holds up her hand to stop me from going any further.

I wouldn't have told Colleen anything else about it, anyway. It was really embarrassing when Danny chased us down to the shore and threw us into the water, although Alli said it didn't bother her, that all was fair in love and war. And, after all, we did put our right hands on Alli's Kotex box and swear we'd never tell anyone.

"The question remains, do we want to sneak into the dance, or go to the male strip show?" Alli says. "Should we, ahem, or should we not, attend the special midnight attraction at the main beach?"

I sneeze, take another drag, and blow smoke toward the ceiling in three imperfect smoke rings. "What've you got in mind? A physical checkup by the light of the silvery moon — or should I bring my flashlight?"

"Hah!" Del holds her thumb and index finger an inch apart. "Those squirts will have dinks smaller than penny firecrackers. Want to bet? Bring along a firefly."

"S'il vous plait, Del," Margot says. "Remember the guy with elephantiasis of the privates that P.S. showed us in her dad's medical book? He wasn't tall. Except for down there, he was a real shrimp."

My sneezing seizure stops me from explaining that the poor man Margot's talking about had a horrible deformity caused by a rare disease. How many guys does Margot think there are that have to push their private parts ahead of them in a wheelbarrow?

"Maybe we ought to see what's what at the main beach at midnight," I say.

"Settled!" Alli says. "Raid's on for midnight sharp. We'll tie their clothes in knots and get a good long inspection."

Del crosses her eyes and twists her bitten fingertips together. "Itty-bitty knots for itty-bitty undies that cover itty-bitty doo-doos," she says, and sighs.

"Ah, ma chere, with the bulge Casanova Danny has in his pants he's a real Drape Prince so he must have something in there to prove it, oui?"

"He might pad it," I say.

"Oui." Del nods her head. "He's probably got a wee wee-wee. Want to bet?"

"Bah!" Colleen says. "Who cares what that so-called Casanova has? Errol Flynn he isn't. He's just a kid. How old is he? Sixteen?"

"And a half," I say. "He's been a dreamboat ever since he was twelve. All the older women like him. Ask anybody at Katepwa. And he likes them too. He's not going to even look at anyone our age, Coll, that's for sure."

"Bah-bah black sheep," Colleen says. "I am not impressed. It's *me* who wouldn't give *him* a second glance."

Alli and I look at each other. I try not to grin. If Colleen isn't impressed with Casanova, she won't even flirt with Van Johnson.

Alli says, "At the witching hour. Naked men."

I cackle and grind my cigarette out in the tin. What I'm hoping is that Van Johnson's smile was as sincere as it seemed, that he sort of liked me.

"Timing's everything on this, P.S., don't be late," Alli calls in a stage whisper as I slip out the back door.

At nine-thirty, I say elaborate goodnights to everyone in the new cottage. It's still quite light outside but dark enough in my sleeping porch for me to light the lamp and pretend I'm reading for awhile before I go to sleep. When I think a suitable length of time has passed, I blow out the lamp and begin the stealthy job of getting off my creaky bed, across the squeaky floor, out the sticking door, and pushing my bike through the bushes up to the road.

I'm back at the cafe at eleven-fifteen.

Colleen isn't with the others. She's in the line-up outside the Katepwa Dance Pavilion with some guy in an air force uniform. She says Fly-boy has already paid her admission, her hand is stamped, she isn't interested in childish pranks, and she refuses to be coaxed away.

We sneak down to the beach at eleven forty-five.

It sounds as if they're already in the water. We drop to the ground, snake our way over the sand to a clump of willows about thirty feet from the water, wiggle through them, and come to rest, still on our stomachs, with our heads under a park bench. We have a clear view.

"Are they stark naked?" Del asks.

"Shh," we all hiss at her.

They're climbing up on the silvery raft. There's a flash of white bums as they run across to the spring board and dive off it. They do windmills in the water. They float on their backs on the silken surface, fountains spin up from their feet, and they sing a chorus of

"Moonlight Bay". Then they swim back to the raft, swing themselves up, and sit on the edge, facing our way.

"Can you see their dinks now?" Del asks.

"Penises," I say.

"Shh, they'll hear us," Alli says. "Take off your sunglasses, dummy."

"I'm blind as a bat without them," Del says. "They're prescription."

"Bats aren't blind at night," I whisper.

Suddenly, Casanova jumps up from the middle of the row and yells, "Ac-cent-tchu-ate the positive, men!"

They all stand up, stretch out their arms to straighten their line, slap their hands down on their bare thighs, and thrust their pelvises forward.

There they are, gleaming in the moonlight like wet Greek statues. Van Johnson doesn't have anything to be ashamed of, lucky him. Boys just don't seem to have the problems becoming men that girls do becoming women. Sure, their voices crack for awhile. So what? Even my brother is counting the days until he can get out of the boys' soprano choir he's in, although he likes singing. The thing is, everything they need to be men, penis, scrotum and testicles, is right there for everyone to see on the outside of their bodies, and all it has to do is grow bigger. If they have to count on a pituitary gland for signals, it looks as if the signal has been given. What I see isn't a medical text illustration. It's flesh. Not pen and ink. Not a photograph with the faces blanked out. Tiny waves lick the shoreline, ticking away the seconds, before I hear Del begin to snicker.

"Do I see diddly-doopity doo-doos?" Del's voice is husky, as if she's got sand in her throat.

"No. You see penises, Del," I say. For me, it's singular. I don't tell her that.

"Shush," Alli cautions. "I think they might know someone's here."

"Come on in, jive-girls, the water's fine," Casanova yells. "Just hang your clothes on a willow limb and don't be afraid of the water." He leads the other guys in a long, coyote-sounding howl.

We stop breathing.

"Okay, men," Casanova shouts. "On your mark! Get set! Let's go get 'em!"

The water explodes in front of the raft. They're torpedoes. Aimed at us. We can see their bodies skimming toward us just under the surface of the water.

We don't stop screaming until we reach the front door of the cafe. "Geeze," I say, spitting a fish fly out of my mouth, "oh, geeze, were we ever set up for suckers."

We flop, panting, into our booth at the back of the cafe.

"Wow!" Del gasps. "Now I know why Addison's called Casanova."

"Mon Dieu! Talk about drape," Margot agrees.

"Maybe that's what keeps him from growing as tall as me," Del says.

Margot giggles. "It's sort of funny, mon vieux. Did you see the way everything's loose and jiggly and bouncing when he runs?"

I'm glad Van Johnson didn't give them anything to chortle about. He had his hands cupped around his private parts when they rose out of the water and started to run toward our bench — a B-cup, at least, I think, and wonder if they sell jock straps sized that way.

"Shut up, you guys," Alli says. "Here they come. Act bored."

Casanova strolls up to our booth, hands in the back pockets of his jeans. "Woof-woof," he says. The rest of his pack, all except Van Johnson who smiles at me, let out some yaps and howls. "If it isn't the jive-girls again," Casanova says. "How's tricks? Any excitement round moonlight bay tonight?"

Alli says, "Nope. None at all. The First's a real fizzle this year." She leans back and gazes up at one of the Coke stains on the beaver-board ceiling. We follow her cue.

Casanova leads the way out the back door of the cafe, whistling "Shoo-Shoo Baby."

Van Johnson is the last one out. He looks over his shoulder and smiles at me; then the screen door slaps shut in my face.

The dance is over. Bill, the Fort Qu'Appelle Playmates' fiddle player who usually unlocks the back door for us after intermission, wasn't there tonight.

We're sitting on the top rail of a double gate, watching cars and trucks full of snuggling couples go by. Alli and I have just propped our feet on the sign, *Linger Longer*, when Casanova pulls up in his dad's Buick Roadmaster.

"Woof!" Casanova says.

"Woof-woof to you, too," Del replies.

"Oui," Margot says. "That goes double for me."

"Don't you ever just say hi?" Alli says. "Woof sounds so childish."

I try to cross my legs and look sultry while I lean forward to see if Van Johnson is in the car. I almost fall off the gate when I see Colleen. She's scrunched-up under Casanova's arm, lighting his cigar.

You've got to ac-cent-tchu-ate the positive, e-lim-in-ate the negative . . . Johnny Mercer is singing on the car radio.

Yes. My dreamboat is sitting in the back seat with the other two guys. There aren't any girls in there with them. That's positive.

But they sit there at our feet, motor running, discussing their plans to drive down to B-Say-Tah Beach where Casanova says there are some student nurses he wants them to meet before they head back to Toronto.

I know that B-Say-Tah translated from Cree means Stay Awhile. Mr. Martell told me that a long time ago.

"See yah sometime, jive-gal," Van Johnson leans out the back window and yells as Casanova revs the motor and they take off in a cloud of dust.

He was just another midnight attraction, I try to tell myself as I ride my bike home. Van Johnson wouldn't be a good match for Hedy Lamarr anyhow. But all the way to the dark cocoon of my sleeping porch, what my bicycle tires say is stay-awhile, stay-awhile, stay-awhile.

The Water Ballet

My *Genuine Hollywood Stars' Bust Builder Kit & Secret Formula Cream* arrived at the Lake Katepwa Store and Post Office on the Ides of July. Alli and I were riffling through movie magazines when Mrs. Rumbles proclaimed the event.

Our postmistress always spoke in whoops, and everything she said sounded like an emergency. She made a noise like a vacuum as she sucked the hot dusty air into her asthmatic lungs, paused, and wailed, "P.S. Scott? *Doctor* P.S. Scott? — beg your pardon. Parcel for you, dear."

"Doctor?" Alli poked me and snickered. "Since when?"

Adding *Dr.* in front of my name on the order form was supposed to reinforce my request for a plain brown wrapper. It hadn't worked. Mrs. Rumbles was holding up a parcel that was wrapped in a reasonable facsimile of the American flag. BUST BUILDER BRINGS SUCCESS TO STARLETS! was printed in jagged, lightning bolt letters between flaming red stripes. The outlines of white stars on a brilliant blue background framed a dazzling display of torso silhouettes portraying the lucky starlets who had developed into bra-bursting movie queens — in ten days or less.

A man standing at the counter wolf-whistled and sang, "Oh, say can you see, by the dawn's early light . . ."

I plunged through the shoppers, snatched the package from Mrs. Rumbles, stuffed it up under my sweat shirt, and dived out the door for my bike.

Inspecting and testing the magic kit in the privacy of my sleeping porch back at our cottage didn't take very long. The looped elastic stretchers that looked like men's suspenders snapped apart on the first good tug, causing a bump to sprout on my breastbone where the apparatus was supposed to develop cleavage. A tube of cream something like the Lanolin ointment my father carried in his medical bag to treat diaper rash — a thick yellow gunk with the same sheepish smell — made my skin break out in raw splotches wherever I got a glob of it to stick to my ribs long enough to rub it around.

It was obvious to me that Hollywood hocus-pocus wasn't going to help me attain the full flowering of womanhood even in ten times ten days. Only a miracle would do that. I would have to go back to praying for the Curse. I chucked the stuff back in the box and kicked the whole works under the bed with the chamber pot. Then I threw myself down on the bed and pulled the comforter up over me.

Why, oh why, hadn't I just been born a seventeen-year locust nymph, a periodical cicada, *Magicicada septendecim*? I could've matured hidden in the ground and, if our biology text had it right, taken anywhere from thirteen to seventeen years to do it. There wouldn't be any need to panic for a few more years. I would simply emerge to shed my nymphal covering and reveal whistle-bait curves to the world when the time was right for me.

Why, oh why, did I have to be the only one who was still flat-chested? It was unnatural. Even minnows had bigger busts than mine. But they didn't have to worry about their shape anyway because they were as sleek as full grown fish. Well, the summer spent in the water with them would be a lot cooler than being covered with earth or sweating it out under a down-filled comforter. And, if I practised my Australian crawl faithfully every day, I'd be able to swim the lake before summer ended. Beginning immediately was essential.

I bounced off the bed and rummaged through the pile of old summer clothes in the corner for my favourite two-piece bathing suit. The bottom half was speckled with tiny holes and the top was like fish net. But who cared? What did I have to cover anyway, I thought. Maybe the magic waters of Katepwa would massage my chest into bloom.

Practising my laps in solitude was what I'd planned; my brother paddling along the shore beside me in our leaky canoe was what I got. My parents said he would cheer me on and save me if I was struck with stomach cramps. That was a joke. When he wasn't exploding into the lake beside me imitating a water bomb, he was creating churning rapids around me with his paddle.

Breathe in and stroke, breathe out and stroke, and flutter-kick, flutter-kick, flutter-kick, *but* — watch out for Bruce's paddle!

My goal was the dock at Hidden Glen, a jackknife turn, and back to our dock without stopping. Half a mile there and half a mile home. The same distance as swimming to the middle of the lake in my first practice.

In-stroke-kick, out-stroke-kick. It looked as if the cupola on Hidden Glen's roof had people in it, watching me. Impossible. I've got water in my eyes. Mr. and Mrs. Glendale have Mr. Martell put the dock out so everything will be ready if their son comes home in the summer. They stay in the city to wait for the second telegram from the War Office apologizing for informing them their son was killed in action.

Flutter-kick, flutter-kick; sure and steady, keep the rhythm. I looked up to gauge my final spurt and almost drowned. Norma Normand and her two older sisters, Nora and Natalie, were standing on the dock at Hidden Glen.

"Hey, P.S.! Need some help? Natalie's got her Gold Lifesaving Medal and Nora and I've got our Bronze," Norma called.

"Hey, that's stopping. Nothing's moving!" Bruce banged his paddle on the water in front of my face and I got a mouthful.

I rolled over on my back in the official rest position for marathon swims, turned to face the dock, and treaded water with my hands. The Normand sisters were wearing checked gingham rompers with pinafore tops; Norma in pink, Nora in yellow and Natalie in mauve. They looked like a row of sweet peas.

"Kick! You've gotta keep kicking," Bruce shouted.

I moved my feet gently. "What're you guys doing at Hidden Glen?" I asked.

"Daddy bought it," Norma said.

"Just for us," Nora added.

"Naturally," Natalie said. "And we've renamed it Normandy Castle. Isn't that romantic?"

Norma smiled down at me and buffed her pink fingernails on the ruffles beside her breasts. "Daddy says this place'll be worth a small fortune when the war's over and the boys come home."

I flopped over and did the jellyfish float until Bruce smacked my bum with the paddle to remind me that only the backfloat was allowed.

"Daddy knew how sick we were of that smelly Y pool." Nora wrinkled her nose and sniffed.

"Naturally. Daddy wanted us to experience something more natural than cement and chlorine," Natalie said.

"So, he bought his three mermaids a summer castle," Norma said. "We've even got a tower. Daddy says it's the only cottage here that does."

They all turned to look up at the cupola and back at me. Their long bronze hair swished back and forth over their shoulders.

Esther Williams triplets, that's what they looked like; a triple exposure on a Coming Attractions poster for *Bathing Beauty*. They held the same pose, smiling widely, showing off their mountainous busts and valleys of cleavage, curves in all the right places down to their painted toenails. Even old spotty-specs Norma, who kept poking me in the back all year in school to ask what was on the blackboard, looked like a pin-up girl with those movie queen sunglasses over her squinty eyes.

"Hey, Sis," Bruce said, "bet I can beat you back home." He started paddling as if a school of piranha was after him.

"Better not get back without me, brat. You'll get killed." I kicked my feet hard enough to back away from the dock.

"Oh no! Don't splash, P.S., we're dry," Nora squealed.

Natalie ran her hands down her torso. "Naturally we are. Cole of California sunsuits aren't made for the water."

"Hey! Don't you dare leave without me, Bruce!" I kicked harder and windmilled my arms behind my head.

"What're *you* wearing?" Norma yanked off her glasses and leaned into the spray instead of shrieking and stepping back with her sisters. "You're half naked!"

I folded my arms across my chest and fluttered my hands like fins. I shouldn't have worn this old suit. The thrash-kick I did to stay afloat put a fountain between us.

"Gee, it sure must be boring hanging around with your kid brother all the time. But don't worry, we'll get things going down here," Norma said. She smiled and adjusted the top of her sunsuit.

"Natalie and Daddy'll jive it up." Nora snapped her fingers and did a few jitterbug steps. "They're going to organize a Katepwa Regatta and Dream Nymph Water Ballet."

"You can be in the ballet if you're a good enough swimmer," Norma called. "Synchronized swimming's a lot harder than just fooling around in the water like you're doing."

"Naturally the Nymphs I pick will have to have really good figures, too," Natalie said.

I turned over and did a racing breast stroke.

"First try-out's here at four o'clock sharp," one of them said. "You're welcome to come. Alli, Delayne and Margot are."

I concentrated on doing an absolutely perfect Australian crawl toward home. I could hear Bruce cheering me on.

It was about four-thirty when I sauntered down to the dock at Normandy Castle. Alli and Del and Margot were already there. We rolled our eyes at each other in our secret what-the-heck greeting. Nobody else showed up for the big try-out.

"Don't forget, we practise at ten a.m. and at two p.m. every single day except Sunday," Natalie said, after telling us she thought she could work with us. "Since I've done all the choreography, naturally I'm the lead swimmer."

"Naturally, Natalie," Nora and Norma said together.

Alli and Del and Margot had to head one way to go home for supper and I had to head the other. We huddled around our bikes on the road at the foot of Thrill Hill behind Normandy Castle before we split up.

"Well? Are we synchronized?" Alli asked.

We all rolled our eyes.

"Let's all join hands and sing that song from the Mikado," Del said. "Since I've made up new words, naturally I'm the lead singer. . .

> Oh, non-Normand sisters are we, are we
> But we do what we do-oh, quite naturally
> Naturally
> Naturally
> Oh, we do what we do-oh
> Quite naturally!"

"Of course, you realize if we practise as much as Natalie wants we'll all turn into nymph-oh-maniacs," I said.

"Naturally!" the others shouted, and we all laughed fiendishly.

Learning to dance in the lake wasn't easy. Norma was right about that. Natalie didn't let us play around during our four hours of practice each day so it wasn't much fun either. I was too waterlogged to even think about doing any more laps in preparation for swimming the lake without stopping. Bruce finally dragged the old canoe up by the cottage and turned it upside-down between two clumps of ash trees. He propped it up on some driftwood and sat under it all day playing Fish by himself with the fortune-telling cards he gave me for my birthday.

Mr. Normand was supposed to be in charge of publicity for The First Annual Katepwa Regatta & Dream Nymph Water Ballet. But all he did was repaint an old B.A. gas sign and print Natalie's name on it in big block letters as the star attraction. He leaned it against the poplar tree outside of the Katepwa Hotel and it made a great substitute for a fire hydrant as far as the beach dogs were concerned.

I talked my father into copying seven Varga Girl drawings from his *Esquire* magazines to make us a poster. It took a bit of convincing to get him to leave off their legs and draw fins instead. But he agreed to do it when I explained that Natalie had dreamed up choreography that had a mythical mermaid theme.

Mrs. Rumbles wheezed and sneezed when I took the poster in to her, but she finally agreed to put it up on the wall over her postal wicket.

Alli's cottage was bedlam on the big day. We chose it as our dressing room because it was so close to our stage at the main beach. There was a crisis when the water turned out to be pea soup with algae down there. Minnows were lying dead in heaps in the turquoise foam along the shoreline. My father and his stage crew of one, my brother, moved our record player and loudspeaker around the point to Stony Cove, where an offshore breeze was keeping the algae stirred up.

Bruce kept running in to inform us of the latest developments. Draped over his head was a towel that he pulled down over his eyes in respect for our modesty.

"Cove's pretty rough and weedy, but there's a bank for the crowd to sit on," he told us.

"*Rhapsody In Blue*'s on the machine, set to go. Has an awful scratch on it, though," he announced.

"Hey! Hurry up, you dames! There's getting to be a huge crowd out there." He almost went through the screen door on his way out that time.

We'd braided and re-braided our hair before pinning the braids across our heads, Heidi-style. Alli looked like Sonja Henie.

Katepwa's Casanova Danny had become Natalie's slave the minute he'd laid eyes on her. She'd sent him to Lebret to get beer for the rest of us, and we dunked our heads in basins of it to prevent wisps of hair from sticking out of our braids. Natalie claimed beer was better than any setting lotion used by Hollywood stars. Of course, she didn't have to use it and have her hair smell like ours did. Natalie, the star, was wearing her hair long and loose and flowing. And Natalie, the star, sent Danny on lots of errands. She sent him to get her father's razor because she thought her armpits needed touching up, more bobby pins, and a lime Stubby for her to sip at her "dressing table". But we still didn't have our costumes. We were in a turmoil about that.

Where was Mr. Normand with the "special deal, imported-from-Hollywood" bathing suits he'd gotten for us from the Army & Navy department store? We kept asking each other that. We hadn't even tried them on. He had decided to have all the suits except Natalie's dyed a deep pink. As the Dream Nymph star, his eldest mermaid ought to be the only one in white, he said. We ran around in circles in our anxiety, dressed in sweat shirts and panties, wafting beer fumes, and tripping over the swim board my father built for us from two six-foot-long, teardrop-shaped pieces of very thin wood glued on the top and bottom of an airtight honeycomb grid.

"Five minutes! Five minutes!" Bruce yelled. "There's a huge crowd! Millions! Five minutes to show time!"

Mrs. Normand rushed in behind Bruce with our suits. We mobbed her. Panic! Strapless wasn't my style. The wired top had nothing to hold it up. Margot had the opposite problem. She couldn't get her large breasts completely squashed into the cups. And Del, because of her long body, had to choose between pulling her suit up over her bust or down over her bum. "Oh well, what the hell," she said, yanking the top up over her nipples. "It's cheeky, but everybody's got a bum — naturally."

"You're on! You're on!" my brother shouted, twirling through the cottage like a whirligig beetle with that white towel wrapped around his head.

It wasn't quite that simple. No curtain. No lights to come up. Just Natalie, in her sparkling white suit and the white net flowers pinned in her long flowing hair, leading us to the edge of our stage through a crowd of about thirty people. We carried the flower-decked swim board behind her like a coffin.

Music! We weren't quite ready. The needle stuck in the scratch and gave us a brief respite before my brother scraped it right across the overture.

We had to cut our opening poses and launch Natalie out on the lake on her gondola. She was arranging herself in a Betty Grable pose among the scratchy net flowers her mother had whipped up, our nerves were taut, and the swim board was lighter than a dragon fly. Natalie almost toppled off from the force of the push we gave her, and we had to swim half-way across to Pelican Point to form a star around her.

We were too far out for the audience to see our star had a wandering sixth point. That was me. I was supposed to swim under water to the swim board and hold it steady while Natalie stood, unfolded her arms to the sun like a nymph being released from the stamen of a carnivorous water lily, and dived gracefully into the deep. Either Natalie slipped — besides being tippy the swim board had several coats of a slick marine paint on it — or my grip wasn't good enough because of some minor stomach cramps I was having. Stage fright, I thought. I suppose Natalie was nervous too. When she bellyflopped with a horrible smack, I swallowed a mouthful of water and my cramps got worse. But I joined the others in doing the two back somersaults Natalie had timed so carefully. Then we waited for Natalie to reappear. One of Alli's braids had fallen down and Nora had a pitchfork of weeds tangled in the pink net flowers on her head. By the time our star finally surfaced, I'd been treading water so long my toes felt webbed.

Natalie led us through the fish hook routine, which was several minutes of floating on our backs, raising one leg at a time in a kick and bend. The music was faint. The rhythm was wrong. We all had to take furtive tugs at our bathing suit tops. In my case, it was impossible to keep it above my waist without devoting one hand to holding it up. One of Margot's breasts sprang free and bobbed up momentarily like a beach ball. She sank from sight in a whirlpool, leaving a wide gap in our chorus line for two intricate maneuvers.

Rhapsody In Blue was too long and too slow. A bad choice. We did ballet versions of the back crawl, front crawl, barrel roll, porpoise dive and chains of somersaults — back ones and forward ones. I had more cramps. It took forever to get to the finale.

At last, it was time for Natalie to lead our V-formation to the shore. It was a marathon swim. The Normand Sisters kept looking back at us and hissing through bared teeth, "Smile-smile-smile! Heads up! Smile!" Natalie said she would pull the swim board back to shore by looping the ring my father had put in its prow over her big toe. That didn't work. The board bobbed past us on its way to Pelican Point. The net flowers were bedraggled and festooned with strands of weeds. It looked like some sort of medieval floating casket.

Close to shore, Natalie was to stay partially immersed in a difficult version she'd dreamed up of the dead man's float, with only her smiling face and her bosom out of the water. We were to form a straight line behind her but do a real dead man's float. It took quite a while for us to get organized.

The music ended too soon. We were in disarray. The Normand Sisters began humming *Rhapsody In Blue* in different keys and at different places in the melody. They hummed faster and faster trying to catch up with each other. That created chaos in our already jerky pacing.

The ending was easier. We had to rise very slowly out of the shallows, lift our arms up over our heads, smile, pirouette without splashing, and, one-two-three — lower our arms as if they were petals unfolding, then watch the star lake nymph rise for her finale. We had to hold our poses until Natalie wiggled a bit like a beautiful mermaid caught on a hook, then rose up, bowed, and stepped onto the shore — imitating Dorothy Lamour's walk in *Star Spangled Rhythm* — revealing to the audience that she had fabulous legs and pretty feet instead of a tail and fins.

Everything went okay until Natalie stood up. What we saw then made us gasp, hoot, and shriek. I heard Mrs. Rumbles gathering enough air into her lungs to wail, "Cover her up! Dear Lord, somebody wrap

THE WATER BALLET 133

something around the girl!'' There were wolf-whistles and guffaws.

Natalie's sleek white sharkskin bathing suit, untouched by Flamingo Pink Rit dye, was completely transparent when wet. We could see the crack in her bum and every freckle, mole and goose pimple, as clearly as if she was stark naked.

"You're *natural*, Natalie," Del howled, and bent over in hysterical laughter which stopped suddenly in a choking sound.

Had the bright pink dye protected us from exposure? For the first time all day our minds and movements were perfectly synchronized. We bowed our heads for personal inspections.

No! Pink cellophane! Absolutely everything that mattered was on full display. Worse, pink dye was bleeding down our legs.

Casanova Danny pushed through the wildly cheering crowd and wrapped Natalie in a green towel. We left her standing there, limp as seaweed, performed an unrehearsed mass racing dive — again perfectly synchronized — and swam faster than fish to Alli's cottage.

It was back at Alli's that I discovered the First Annual Katepwa Regatta and Dream Nymph Water Ballet hadn't been a complete fiasco for *me*. It had been a personal triumph, a new beginning. I'd been blessed with the Curse — finally! That's why the dye running down my legs was so red, as red as a red, red rose. That's why I had those lovely little cramps.

Unless that phony Hollywood bust-building stretcher could be turned into a sanitary belt, who needed it? My chest would bloom quite naturally. It felt like it was swollen already. I had shed my nymphal covering in the green-green waters of Lake Katepwa and stepped forth a WOMAN! — or, at least, a girl with the right things happening to become a woman.

I'm going to have breasts at last, I thought. God bless the miracle of my uterus.

Webs

It's early May, 1933, one of those hot humid mornings in Tuscaloosa that are sticky as glue, and my father is all dressed up in his new grey and white seersucker suit. Lily tucks a hibiscus blossom in his lapel buttonhole; a bright red trumpet, she says, on account of the occasion. He's on his way to the Druid City Hospital to get my mother and new baby brother.

Our front porch is a Welcome Home stage. The kitchen band my father arranged for is tuning up their pots and pans, glasses and jugs. The black man wearing a top hat runs wooden spoons up and down different sized washboards.

I sit on the wicker porch swing right where Lily plunked me and said to stay put or else. I'm not supposed to get a speck of dirt on my dress. Great Aunt Ginger won the Dixieland World Champion Smocking Ribbon for this dress at the Alabama State Fair. It's too small for me now. After Lily helps me out of it, I'll have smock-marks on my chest, back, and around my upper arms. But Lily wants me to look sweet as pecan pie for my brother's homecoming. She says it won't do me a bit of good to fret about my dress being a mite tight.

Lincoln, the man who does the cleaning at my father's lab, is the leader of the kitchen band. He tells me that today I look as pretty as Miss Shirley Temple. I twist one of the ringlets Lily made with my mother's curling iron and ask if he'll please get his band to play the spider song my daddy always whistles.

The band members know the words:

> Itty bitty spider
> up the water spout.
> Down comes a raindrop
> to wash the spider out.
> Out comes the sunshine
> and dries up the rain.
> Itty bitty spider's
> up the spout again.

They harmonize, like everyone does at the revival tent Lily takes me to sometimes when she says she just has to cut loose and let her voice fly up to the Lord. Then they sing it in rounds and I join in.

Lily doesn't sing a note. She thrums the wicker behind my back with her blunt grey fingernails. "Honeychile," she leans over and whispers in my ear, "them nasty spider's gone get your daddy one day, less you be cautious. You juss askin for trouble singin so sweet bout one."

I shiver and clamp my mouth shut.

I'm afraid of spiders now, dead or alive. Lily knows my secret. She came along with us last summer when we went up to Canada to stay at my grandmother's lake cottage. Everyone said it was the driest year in Saskatchewan history. The uncle who took over my grandfather's farm kept complaining that his wheat wasn't heading out worth a goddamn. Mother and Grandma and Lily killed every spider they could find to bring on rain. Lily was towelling me dry after a swim when the fat brown spider crawled right up to me. I stamped on it. The spider squished under the sole of my rubber bathing slipper like a burnt marshmallow. I jerked my foot up and saw spiderlings race out of the mush toward dark corners of the veranda like tiny red sparks from a dead sun. Lily started to sing "Didn't It Rain", then she saw the look on my face. My uncle cleaned up the mess with his cigarette papers, muttering while he did it about me causing cloudbursts that would rust out his bumper crop. I threw up on Lily's lap. She remembers.

When we hear the roadster's horn and other car horns honking back over on University Boulevard, the band plays "My Blue Heaven".

"Menfolk an sons!" Lily says, fluffing up the puffed sleeves of my dress.

My father has the baby tucked along one arm like a football and his other arm around my mother's waist as they dance toward us. My mother is wearing the georgette dress she got married in. She keeps it wrapped in tissue paper for special occasions. Lily likes to try the dress on and twirl through the house in it when my mother is out. It's our secret, I promised. She made me spit in my shoe and swear never to tell.

"Hey, lil booger," Lily greets the baby when my father hands him to her. She cuddles him to her thin body and looks my mother over, head to toe. "Welcome home, Mam," she says. "You lookin mighty fine, Mizz Vee, though that ole dress doan do nothin to accentuate it. It juss doan look good on you no more. No Mam, it sure nough doan."

Mother does a few steps of the Charleston and the dipping hem swishes around her ankles. "Still fits like a glove, Lily. But it'll be yours when I can part with it," she says. "I promise."

"Hey, Miss Tuscaloo," my father says, scooping me off the swing and setting me on his shoulders. "How do you like your new baby brother? Some handsome little man, isn't he?"

I rest my chin on my father's head and look down at the baby. "Uh-huh," I say. He looks like my Wetums doll. "Daddy, can I go with you to see your spiders again?" I ask. "Just you and me?"

My father's lab is painted cream and green and it smells like a hospital. We scrub our hands at the sink, and my father gives me a white lab coat to put on. He rolls up the sleeves for me. I try, but I can't reach the patch pockets to dig my hands down in them like he does.

There are two long shelves of black widow spiders in oblong jars for him to show me. Cards with their histories on them are held upright on the lids. My father has been studying black widow spiders for as long as I can remember: collecting specimens, trying to breed them, taking venom from their poison sacs and injecting it into his lab animals.

"Rats and mice die, just like that," he tells me, snapping his fingers. "My guinea pigs get quite ill, but most survive. Rabbits, cats and dogs aren't seriously affected. I suspect they build up an immunity to the widow's venom."

"Lily says people die if they get bitten."

"No, they don't. Hardly ever. Dr. Bogen studied four hundred cases of documented black widow spider poisoning from 1720 to 1931 and only twelve of the people died."

Twelve! I start counting: Daddy and me and my mother and Lily and my baby brother and Great Aunt Ginger, Grandma and all our kinfolk in Canada like —

"Not that you want to play around asking to be bitten," my father says. "But a widow's web is easy as pie to recognize. Here's a perfect example. See this?"

I look in the jar he points at.

"See how messy it is? How the threads are all helter-skelter, crisscrossing at various angles and planes?"

"Uh-huh," I say.

"A widow usually builds her web in a crevice or corner. That's so she can retreat in a hurry, sometimes through a poorly formed tunnel of silk, like here." He taps his finger on the glass.

"Oh!" I cry, as the spider darts toward it.

My father chuckles. "She's cranky, not used to living in a glass jar yet. Probably thought I was going to steal some of her web. You know why, Miss Tuscaloo? Spider silk is considered to be of a much finer quality than a silkworm's. If I collected enough of it, maybe I could get a pretty dress made for you out of spider silk."

I don't say anything.

"Black widows spin especially fine silk. Do you know what it's used for? The cross sections in telescopic sights. A single strand is as strong as a steel wire of equivalent thickness. That's why the wicked widow can weave a death cradle for victims many times her size. See what this vicious little lady has trapped in hers? Lincoln swept a mouse nest out from under the stairs yesterday."

He lifts me up so my eyes are level with a jar on the top shelf. Up near the lid, a pink baby mouse is suspended in a silk shroud. The spider is on the mouse's stomach. I shut my eyes, swallow hard.

"She's been having a feast sucking its juices ever since we dropped it in there. Lincoln didn't think her web would hold it. Don't worry, the mouse didn't suffer. The first quick nip from that nasty lady shot in a venom that's fifteen times deadlier than a rattlesnake's."

10:45 A.M., Sunday, November 12, 1933

He gently grasps the black widow spider by its abdomen with a pair of splinter forceps and places it on the little finger of his left hand.

The spider bites instantly.

Spider Number 111.33 has not been fed for fifteen days. It is an active healthy specimen that he captured in a rock pile at the edge of the cotton field across from our house on Hackberry Lane. Its bulbous abdomen is half an inch in length and in width at the posterior, glossy black, and has on its underside the characteristic adult female marking of a red hourglass.

The subject of the experiment is age 32, five feet eleven inches in height, weighs 168 pounds (76.2 kg), is athletically inclined and in excellent health. He played quarterback on a winning team at McGill University and has recently won the University of Alabama Faculty of Medicine singles tennis cup. His reaction to bee stings and mosquito bites is normal.

He permits the spider to bite him for ten seconds.

The spider twists its cephalothorax from side to side as though to sink the claws above its mouth deeper into his flesh. Venom is being discharged through the tiny openings near the tip of each claw. He records the sensation as being like the prick of a sharp hot needle, accompanied by a localized burning that increases in intensity during the biting period.

After he removes the spider and replaces it in its jar, a drop of clear fluid, slightly streaked with brown, remains at the site of the bite. He leaves this untouched for one minute before wiping it off with a cotton pledget. No definite marks of skin puncture can be seen with the naked eye or with low magnification.

The lymphatic absorption of the poison takes fifty minutes. He makes detailed notes on how the pain spreads and worsens.

An explosive onset of widespread muscular pains and profound shock occurs as the venom begins to circulate in his bloodstream. His two student assistants take over the record-keeping.

His speech is jerky, respiration rapid and laboured. Sharp brisk expirations are followed by loud grunts. His pulse is rapid, uncountable, weak and thready. The heart sounds are slow, his abdomen rigid, boardlike.

He asks to be taken to the Veterans Hospital where he has arranged for use of the electrocardiograph machine if he needs it.

There is a flushed trembly feeling in his legs and he is unable to straighten up or walk. Lincoln appears in the lab doorway and offers to carry him to the car.

The hospital is three miles from the campus, normally a fifteen-minute drive, but there are Sunday strollers and drivers to dodge. Lincoln rides on the running board of the car, yelling, "Lordy-Lord! Clear the path! The good Doc's done got his self bit by a red spotted coal black lady! Lord, we gone save him! We gone do it, Lord willin.''

It is torture for him to lie still on his back while two electrocardiograms are made. They do not show any heart damage, but his skin is cold and clammy, his lips are contracted by pain, causing his mouth to assume an oval shape. At his request, the assistants run a hot bath and Lincoln lowers him into it, which, he is able to state, brings him some relief from the pain.

The attending physician first sees him at this stage of the spider poisoning and writes his observations in the record: I found the patient in excruciating pain, gasping for breath, and reclining in a tub of very warm water. I do not recall having seen more abject pain manifested in any other medical or surgical condition.

For more than forty-eight hours, the clinical chart of his respiratory rate, blood pressure and pulse is a series of jagged lines. Uh-huh, he remarks when it's shown to him, the widow's web.

On November 15, three days after the bite and thirteen days before his thirty-third birthday, he has almost completely recovered from the poisoning. Rheumatoid pains in his legs and feet, a feeling of shakiness when he stands or walks, are his chief complaints. The doctor agrees with his decision to leave the hospital on condition he goes home by ambulance.

It isn't porch weather for his homecoming. Nobody minds.

My brother is in a brushed cotton bunting with a hood that has rabbit ears on it. I'm cosy as a kitten in my Chesapeake Railroad overalls and a heavy pullover sweater my grandmother up in Canada sent to me. Lily has my father's Harris tweed jacket on over her long-sleeved uniform. She holds my brother on her hip and I stand beside them at the top of the porch steps. Behind us, the men in Lincoln's kitchen band are keeping warm by taking turns tap-dancing up and down the length of the porch.

My mother, who says her nice thick Saskatchewan blood has gotten thin living in Alabama, is all bundled up in what she calls her "snow angel cloak", a long butterfly cape that Great Aunt Ginger knit for her out of white angora. She's waiting down at the end of the sidewalk with Lincoln and two news reporters.

When we see the ambulance cross McFarland Avenue on the far side of the cotton field, Lincoln holds the eggbeater up over his head and spins the blades to signal the band to start playing. They strike up with "Just A Closer Walk With Thee". Lily jiggles my brother on her hip and lets loose with the words, hums, then sings words I can't understand except for the hallelujahs.

The attendants lift my father out of the ambulance on a stretcher. He refuses to stay on it. Mother walks on one side of him, holding his hand, Lincoln on the other side, his big black hand splayed on my father's arm like a giant spider. Their smiles are watermelon slices.

The reporters walk backwards toward us, squatting and stretching to take pictures with their cameras, flashbulbs exploding. The band plays the spiritual faster to match their quickening steps. The old man who blows in the jugs makes them sound like trumpets and bugles. They must be able to hear Lily up in Canada, I think.

My father sits down in one of the plantation rockers. Mother runs inside for a blanket to tuck over his knees. After the band plays "When The Saints Go Marching In", the reporters ask questions.

Did he know black widow spider venom is fifteen times deadlier than a rattlesnake's?

Yes, my father says, in equal amounts it's supposed to be. He knew that. And now he believes it's true. He smiles.

Why take such a risk letting one bite you then, Doctor?

That's what I want to know too, but my brother starts to howl and then Lily grabs my arm and hauls me along with her when she takes him into the house.

Mother lets me help paste clippings in a scrapbook. She reads the headlines out loud: PROFESSOR LETS SPIDER BITE HIM, SUFFERS 3 DAYS AGONY; CANADIAN M.D. SUBMITS TO AGONIZING EXPERIMENT TO AID SCIENCE.

"Beg pardon, Mizz Vee," Lily says, turning from the sink where she's singeing pinfeathers off a chicken with torches made from discarded parts of the newspapers. "Juss seem to me he bin askin for agony, foolin with them red spotted poison spiders — stead of devotin his self to you'all, considerin."

"You read my mind, Lily," Mother says. "But this time the foolish fly was lured into the spider's parlour and came out a hero. *The Tuscaloosa News* says he was braver than the Mississippi convicts who were guinea pigs for the St. Louis physicians trying to find out how sleeping sickness is transmitted."

"Spect menfolk wantin free got reason nough to let their selves be guinea pigs. Ain't no reason the doctor got to go seekin no glory that way, ask me," Lily says.

"Or me," Mother agrees.

I don't say anything. The Associated Press account of the experiment I'm pasting in the book has lots of pictures of my father and his spiders. Mother says it was chosen as one of the ten best human interest stories of the year. I can't help thinking it's sort of exciting to have a father who's famous.

But later, my father hears that he won't be getting a research job he wanted because he's too famous.

Too much publicity about his work with red spotted coal black ladies, he tells my mother, his research should have been published in one of the medical journals first. He says the A.M.A. won't support doctors who do experiments on themselves, they think it's unscientific, if not downright foolish.

Well, my mother says, well.

My father says he's sick of pathology and never having any patients who can talk back to him. He says he's fed up with watching black widow spiders eat their mates.

Good, my mother says, get rid of those damn spiders.

He tells her he loves teaching and learning, but that life is too slow and easy for him in the South, that before long he'll be able to do what he's doing in his sleep and he's afraid he'll get to enjoy that. He says she knows how easily he can be seduced, then he puts his arms around her and gives her a kiss.

Well, my mother says, now what?

He wants to use the savings they've banked in Canada to go north and study surgery, radiology, learn everything he can about the diagnosis and treatment of cancer — seek a new challenge.

They decide to move home, home to Canada.

Home, my father explains to me, isn't necessarily a person's birthplace. He says my brother and I will always have close ties to Tuscaloosa, to Alabama. Webs spun by the Deep South around her sons and daughters, he says, are even stronger than black widow spider silk.

It's almost midnight, November 13, 1948.

I've come down to the dark corner of our basement to look for my father's black widow spiders in the Tuscaloosa trunk. Underneath the old Alabama clothes my mother has saved, there's a large maroon box full of spiders suspended in glass slides. I discovered them when I was nine years old soon after we'd moved to Regina. They wait with hooked claws ready to strike, their mouths open to suck my body dry if I make a false move or shift my eyes even a fraction while I dig down into the trunk for them. Whenever my parents stayed out late and I was left in charge, I'd lie in my bed too scared to move a muscle, listening and listening, afraid that the spiders had come alive, shattered the glass slides, and were creeping up the stairs to get me. Sometimes I had to force myself to come down here to make sure the spiders were only specimens trapped on Wratten M Dry Plate slides and not like the darting spiders my father kept in the jars in his lab.

I shudder.

Sleet pings on the window pane. The cement floor is an ice floe. I don't care if I get chilblains and double pneumonia from being down here in my bare feet and pyjamas. There has to be a reason.

My father is dead. He was buried this afternoon, fifteen days before his forty-eighth birthday. Hearing the earth fall on his coffin was the worst part: the thud of dirt frozen to rocks. But I didn't cry. I won't cry.

He didn't suffer, my mother says. It was so quick he didn't feel any pain. She keeps repeating this.

I saw my father have his first heart attack. She must have forgotten that. He shouted, "Hey!", fell down on the rug all hunched up, and he writhed around, pounding his chest with his fists, grunting, gasping for breath through a fish-shaped mouth.

By the time the doctor arrived, he was lying on the chesterfield, the pain almost gone. They decided he'd had a severe attack of indigestion. A year later he had another attack, far worse, and their diagnosis changed.

The three-month recuperation after his third heart attack was almost over. He was back at the cancer clinic part-time.

A soft wet snow fell on his last morning. He and Mother stood for a long time at the kitchen window admiring the way the prairie grass looked with puffs of snow on it. He said it would be easy to mistake the prairie for a cotton field ready for picking. Mother says he was whistling the spider song when he went upstairs after lunch for the prescribed nap he hated taking.

Mother had just started doing the dishes when he called her name. She ran up to their bedroom, the sopping wet dishrag still clutched in her hand. There's a white mark on the bedside table where she dropped it.

He looked as if he'd fallen asleep just as something surprised him, Mother says, there was a startled look on his face and his mouth was open as if he'd just exclaimed, "Oh!" She gave him mouth-to-mouth resuscitation, phoned the doctor, the ambulance, a friend who used to be a nurse.

There was nothing anyone could do. It was too late.

Fifteen years too late.

A newspaper article said his premature death could have resulted from cardiac damage caused when he allowed a black widow spider to bite him to test the effects of its venom on the human heart.

"No!" Mother shouted when she read it. "Won't those damn spiders ever be forgotten!" She crumpled the newspaper and hurled it across the living room. "That's not why he let that spider bite him. It's not!"

"Why did he?" I asked her. "Why?" I wanted to scream questions at her. Did he let it bite him to show how brave he was? Did you want him to do it so he'd be a hero? Didn't he care if he died? Did he love those spiders more than us?

"He wanted to know how to diagnose and treat black widow spider poisoning. He thought one bite might give him immunity to others. But he said he didn't have the courage to finish the experiment by letting himself be bitten again to prove it. Courage?" Mother looked at me. "Well, maybe it was, but it was foolish too. There was something so damn seductive about those bloody little coal black widows."

We stared at each other. I had sometimes boasted to my friends that my father was the famous scientist who had discovered a cure for black widow spider poisoning. Did she know that?

The smell of camphor begins to burn my nostrils as I get closer to uncovering the maroon box. I jump and almost scream out loud when mothballs roll out of my father's old red McGill sweater. The M on the front is missing. I snipped it off and wore the sweater to school when I was in Grade 9. It was right in fashion, big and long enough to let just a fringe of Blackwatch tartan pleats show beneath it. I used to sneak out of the house in it so no one would know I'd been snooping in the Tuscaloosa trunk.

My father's old seersucker suit is wrapped in whispery tissue paper on top of the maroon box, the last piece of clothing. Mother gave her wedding dress to Lily to be married in so it's not in here. I reach down to lift out the suit. My skin crawls. I swat at a tickle on my neck. My fingers tingle. I grit my teeth, shut my eyes, and shove the suit off the box.

Something is watching me. The spider.

An enlarged black and white photograph of it lies face-up on top of the maroon box. It's labelled in white ink in my father's neat printing: *Spider #111.33 — The Culprit! — 11/28/33*.

He took its picture on his thirty-third birthday. He used red ink on its bloated belly to colour the hourglass.

I tear the photograph into bits.

Crying now, I grab the heavy maroon box out of the trunk, yank off the lid, and smash the spider slides, one by one, on the cold grey cement floor.

Acknowledgements

Grateful acknowledgement is made by the author to the editors of the anthologies in which earlier versions of seven stories in this book first appeared: "Best Kept Secrets" appeared in *More Saskatchewan Gold;* "Playboy" in *Sundogs* and *100% Cracked Wheat;* "Vital Statistic" and "In The Middle" in *The Canadian Children's Annual;* "Second Sight" in *The Old Dance;* "The Lookout Stone" in *Saskatchewan Gold;* "The Water Ballet" in *100% Cracked Wheat.* "Webs" was published in the April 1988 issue of *Prism international.*

The talking dolls dialogue in "Star Bright" was originally prepared by the author for a CBC Radio broadcast and it later appeared in *Chatelaine.* The experiment described in "Webs" is based on a paper published by the author's father, A.W. Blair, M.D., in *The Archives of Internal Medicine* (December 1934, Volume 54). The Mother's Day card in "In The Middle" is a slightly edited version of one written by Barbara Krause Sanders, the author's middle daughter. The diary entry in "Just Another Midnight Attraction" is from *Freshie* (Potlatch, 1981).

"Star Bright", "Playboy", "Vital Statistic", "In The Middle" and "The Water Ballet" (in a version that included "Just Another Midnight Attraction") won awards in Saskatchewan Writers Guild literary competitions. "Webs" was awarded honorable mention in the *Prism international* 1987 short story competition.

Pat Krause was born in Tuscaloosa, Alabama, where her father was on the medical faculty of the University of Alabama. When her family returned to Canada in 1934, they lived in Winnipeg, Indian Head, Toronto, and, in 1939, moved back to her father's home town of Regina, where Pat presently lives with her husband Frank. Pat spends summers at a family cottage in the Qu'Appelle Valley and some of her stories are set there. Following fifteen years devoted to four children and being a happy housewife, Pat returned to the paid work force as a part-time apartment rental agent with an office in her broom closet. Since then, she has worked setting up and administering a medical tape library for doctors, as a writer-commentator for CBC Radio, as creative writing co-ordinator and workshop leader at the Saskatchewan School of the Arts at Fort San, and as a communications officer at the University of Regina. Pat is now writing as fast as she can, full-time.

Best Kept Secrets is Pat's first collection of short stories. *Freshie,* a novel that won a Government of Saskatchewan literary award in manuscript, was published in 1981. She won the first W.O. Mitchell Bursary to apprentice as a writer and writing instructor at the Saskatchewan School of the Arts in 1975, was awarded the 1981 City of Regina writing grant, and received an Individual Assistance Grant from the Saskatchewan Arts Board in 1984.

Pat is presently working on her second novel, *Southern Relations.*

"Sunday Sweaters and Orson Welles", the cover art reproduced on *Best Kept Secrets,* is by Elyse Yates St. George, a Saskatoon painter and poet.

Fiction from Coteau Books

Other fiction from Coteau Books is listed below. For a complete list of publications — fiction, poetry, drama, criticism, humour and children's literature — please write to Suite 209, 1945 Scarth St., Regina, Saskatchewan S4P 2H2.

Fiction from Coteau Books

Pat Krause, *Best Kept Secrets.* Hilarious and moving stories from a Regina writer. $21.95 (cl)/$8.95 (pbk), Fall 1988.

Sky High: Stories from Saskatchewan. Twenty-four stories from Saskatchewan writers, edited by Geoffrey Ursell. $5.95 (pbk), Fall 1988.

The Old Dance: Love Stories of One Kind or Another. Thirty short stories that examine love, edited by Bonnie Burnard. $4.95 (pbk), Fall 1986.

More Saskatchewan Gold. Imaginative and masterful short stories from Saskatchewan writers, edited by Geoffrey Ursell. $4.95 (pbk), Fall 1984.

Sharon Butala, *Queen of the Headaches.* This collection was nominated for the Governor-General's Award. $5.95 (pbk), Fall 1985.

Veronica Eddy Brock, *The Valley of Flowers: A Story of a TB Sanatorium.* A popular novel about the experiences of a young girl confined to a TB sanatorium during the forties. $5.95 (pbk), Fall 1987.

Barbara Sapergia, *Foreigners.* A sensitive portrayal of a Romanian immigrant family on the Prairies at the turn of the century. $4.95 (pbk), Fall 1983.

The McCourt Fiction Series

Bonnie Burnard, *Women of Influence.* Volume 5 in the McCourt Fiction Series. Fourteen compelling and insightful short stories. $21.95 (cl)/$8.95 (pbk), Fall 1988.

Dianne Warren, *The Wednesday Flower Man*. McCourt Fiction Series 4. Witty and whimsical fiction. $16.95 (cl)/$8.95 (pbk), Fall 1987.

Connie Gault, *Some of Eve's Daughters*. McCourt Fiction Series 3. Unusual stories in an eclectic range of styles. $16.95 (cl)/$8.95 (pbk), Spring 1987.

Reg Silvester, *Fish-Hooks*. McCourt Fiction Series 2. Thirteen surprising stories with a sense of the bizarre. $6.00 (pbk), Fall 1984.

Robert Currie, *Night Games*. McCourt Fiction Series 1. Poignant stories about adolescence in the fifties. $7.00 (pbk), Fall 1983.